A Boy Fighter With
ANDREW JACKSON

By
H. C. THOMAS

Illustrated by
HENRY E. VALLELY

WHITMAN PUBLISHING COMPANY
RACINE, WISCONSIN

TABLE OF CONTENTS

"Go," Lee Baird Shouted to Venus

A Boy Fighter With ANDREW JACKSON

CHAPTER ONE

A DISTINGUISHED VISITOR

The two-year-old bay filly stood listening with cocked ears while Lee Baird again explained the signals he was trying to teach her. Venus watched her boy master with impatience but permitted him to stroke her soft muzzle while he talked and now and again to reach back and smooth his hand under her neck.

"Remember," he said, "in a race there'd be so much noise from other horses and people watching that you mightn't hear my voice. That's why you must learn signals from my heels and the way I shift weight."

Venus tossed her head impatiently. She pawed, eager to go speeding once more across the stump-dotted Tennessee frontier farm.

"I'm never going to use a whip on you—that's for a horse that hasn't been trained as you have," Lee explained. "When I want you to go faster, I'll lean forward. If I press my heels, it means faster yet. If

I kick you—then," he told the horse earnestly, "you let go and fly! Do you understand?"

He thought Venus did, and grinned fondly. Lee's grin, his father said, "used his whole face." His mother, while she lived, had called it "sunny." It was a friendly, winning grin, with crinkling at the corners of his eyes while the corners of his mouth stretched sideways. It went with his tousled sandy hair and his lanky six feet in gray homespun shirt, deerskin trousers, and rough frontier boots.

Venus rubbed her forehead against his chest as if suggesting they had enough of talk. He pulled her ears affectionately.

"All right, we'll start now." He glanced across the hill at the forlorn-looking one-room cabin of logs that was his home. There was no sign yet of his father's return from Nashville where Adam Baird yesterday had taken their tobacco and bales of cotton for safety from the bushwhacker thieves who prowled this lonely country. Lee thought his father would not get home before sundown, an hour away.

He tossed the home-made reins over Venus's ears, stepped to her left shoulder, and vaulted on her back. The reins were his only equipment, and Lee had never sat a saddle, though he had ridden since he was five years old and now was almost seventeen. Few farmers could afford saddles except—well, a man like Judge Andrew Jackson, whom his father talked about so much. Judge Jackson had been an Indian fighter and a senator and he was Tennessee's most prominent citizen; and of course his famous racer, Truxton, probably wore a saddle.

Lee smiled reflectively. It would be exciting if he could try Venus against Truxton some time! But—no use dreaming, for of course such a race would never be held.

He turned Venus and looked ahead. His training course was not even a path. He simply started here at the edge of the gloomy pine forest, guided Venus among the stumps, and on reaching the grassy draw swung right a straight half-mile or so to the creek.

He straightened, lifting his reins. The filly tensed. He waited to make sure she always would remember about being ready. "Go!" Lee shouted, and gave her a light kick.

She shot forward as if released by a spring. Down the slope they whirled, twisting this way and that to avoid stumps. He imagined a competitor racing beside them—that the other horse was forging ahead. Lee slacked his reins, and Venus instantly sped faster.

"Gently, now. Don't get excited. That fellow can't beat us!"

He felt her calm to his words. They shot away from the last stumps and onto the meadow floor where grass rose over her ankles. Her hoofs were drumming, her beautiful mane tossing, her ears cocking alertly forward, then expectantly back.

Leaning forward, Lee felt her stride lengthen. As the imaginary horse beside them again pulled ahead he clasped his legs tighter on the filly's barrel. Venus did not respond, and he frowned. He gave her a light heel-tap.

Now she understood! She spurted ahead so eagerly that he had to hold her in check. The meadow swam under them. That broken tree marking the far bank of the creek whirled rapidly nearer.

He slackened his reins, at the same instant giving a hard, staccato kick. "Now run, Venus!" he cried.

And run she did, as if she had been trotting before! She seemed almost flying. The August sun beat down on boy and horse whizzing across the fading-green meadow, the boy leaning and talking to her, the filly reaching out with her muzzle, her hoofs seeming all a-scramble as they thrust ground behind her.

Without hesitation Venus leaped soaring over the creek. She would have continued her mad run but gradually he pulled her in. When he stopped and turned her around, she shook her head, angry that the trial was over.

Lee made her walk slowly back through the creek. "Venus, you never ran like that! You're a racer—a real racer!"

Someone was shouting. His brows gathered as he sighted two men up near the log house. One, the shorter, stockier of them, was gesturing for Lee to come. That was his father, back from his overnight trip to Nashville to store their produce safely. The other man was quite tall and thin. His beaver hat shone in the sun and even at that distance Lee saw that his clothes were very finely tailored.

He trotted Venus up to them, stopped her and slid off, grinning widely. His father advanced and clapped his shoulders.

"How that filly flew! You've made a secret of her, lad—you kept it from me!" He laughed.

Lee was beaming and proud. "Faith, I said she's a wonder, didn't I? Only I wanted to surprise you, Father, what a wonder she is!"

Adam Baird, woodsman, militiaman, farmer, was a cheery companion. Perhaps he was not quite so cheery since the death of his wife three years ago, shortly after the family moved onto these untamed hundred and sixty acres. But he always worked with a will because he loved the frontier where, he said, a man must be strong, honest, and willing in order to survive.

"Keep busy as the squirrel, strong as the bear, and honest as the deer," he often said. "Then men'll respect ye—yes, and animals, too."

The visitor stepped nearer Venus. " 'Tis plain you've made your filly want to run, lad. That's the best reason of all for a horse to be speedy. I've heard of your Venus." He ran his hand over her chest. "She's a beauty, sure enough."

Lee wondered who the gentleman was; the next thing the stranger said told him. "She has a good chest, yet narrow like Truxton's. And long hind legs —they're what push her so fast. Three-quarters of a horse's weight is on the back legs. So they need to be powerful." He smiled at Lee's continued stare.

"Sir, could you be—"

"I forgot," Adam Baird said hastily. " 'Tis Judge Jackson, Lee, honoring us for supper. My old militia commander—you know."

Indeed he knew, for his father was always telling how Andrew Jackson had been a poor boy like him only a few years ago. He had applied his head and his hands and had become eminent without help from anyone.

"Some day," his father said, "I'll want Old Hickory to look at you and say what you're worth. If he gives you a bit of advice—" Mr. Baird always paused impressively—"then you follow it. For Andy Jackson knows men and horses, and he knows 'em thorough, I'll warrant ye!"

The visitor had looked Venus over very carefully. He took a snuff box from a vest pocket and put a pinch of the powder in each nostril, sniffing. From his cuff he drew a large handkerchief and dusted his rather sharp nose. "Well, Lee, how will you trade?"

"Eh?" he said, startled.

"Want to sell your filly? With good care I could

make her win races."

Lee backed against Venus defensively. "No sir, General Jackson, I—"

"He's Judge Jackson now," his father corrected.

"No, Adam," the narrow-faced visitor smiled. "I'm recently a general again, as I was about to explain. But Lee, you don't care to sell Venus here? With the money you could perhaps go to school."

Lee knew how his father wanted him to be educated and make something of himself. And he wanted to study law, too. But—sell Venus?

"Sir, I—I just couldn't. I've got to have her!" he said earnestly.

"I understand, lad. Well then," General Jackson suggested with a twinkle in his keen gray eyes, "suppose we think of matching your filly with my Truxton? D'ye think Venus'd win?"

"With more training she might," he replied loyally.

The men laughed. "No horse can beat Truxton, Lee," his father said.

"Some horse'll beat him some day. Sooner or later, there's always a faster horse."

"You're right, lad. But Truxton's in his prime, and I'd risk all I own on him against any four-legged creature. Well, you'll want to rub down your filly."

Lee took Venus to the three-walled barn where General Jackson's roan was already stabled, and busied himself rubbing her carefully while he talked approvingly about her good run. He gave her a half-measure of recently-shocked oats, just for the flavor, and promptly she ignored him to munch them greedily. But when he had flung the be-patched blanket on her and was leaving the barn, she turned her head with that odd look which, he vowed, showed amusement.

"Good horse," he said. "Faith, if I had money I'd bet it on you over Truxton any day!"

When he entered the house, General Jackson had opened his long-tailed black coat, pulled off one tight boot, filled his clay pipe, and was smoking and talking comfortably. Adam Baird had an earthenware pot of beans cooking in the embers of the log fire while, hugging a flitch of bacon to his chest, he cut strips from it with his hunting knife.

General Jackson nodded to Lee and kept on chatting with Mr. Baird. Lee found a stool and sat on it with his back against the wall, listening. The open door showed an orange sunset beyond the bleak hills and it was cozy here watching the men and hearing them talk. Besides, he wanted to study Andrew Jackson, whom his father considered a man to imitate if one wanted to be successful.

There was something about his face with its narrowness, and his straight slash of mouth, and his quick, piercing eyes that suggested an eagle. His talk came in blunt words and short sentences. He said something and was done, and there could be no mistaking what he meant. He did not look robust, yet he was wiry and tough. And the way he could not sit still but kept shifting position and gesturing proved that neither his mind nor body could long be at rest.

He complained to Mr. Baird "—posse after posse, but the sheriff can't seize 'em. Of course, we'll hang those bushwhackers eventually. They've killed freely and robbed farmers of all they possessed. 'Tis a shame, I say, in this year 1813! When's Tennessee to become civilized?"

"Aye, General. A man sweats and starves to cut a farm out of this wilderness, then in a matter of moments some scoundrelly bushwhacker filches his all—and his very life to boot." Adam Baird's look went to the long deer rifle resting on horns over the fireplace. "Such ruffians should be shot on sight."

"You'll be wise, Adam, to continue taking your produce to Nashville so's not to lose it if those varmints ever pay you a visit."

"Aye. We've property there now, safe in Terry's warehouse. We must think of keelboating it to New Orleans come fall."

General Jackson nodded. "The bloodiest of the bushwhackers'd gladly murder women and children before breakfast. He's cruel as a fox and as hard to catch. They call him Deerhide."

"Deerhide? Aye, I've heard of that scoundrel."

"He's been seen in this district of late, so never be

far from your gun. Because if he and his band did call here, they might be angry that you've moved your tobacco and cotton to safety."

"And a few hides as well. Yes, we'll keep alert. The beans are ready," he added. "We keep 'em half-cooked so our hunger needn't wait so long. Plates, Lee. And find a napkin for General Jackson from your mother's trousseau that she brought from Virginny. Of course we can't offer the fine service you have at your mansion, sir," he apologized.

"Tut, man. The smell's got me eager. Remember, Adam, times we were forced to gnaw bark in our soldiering days? And thought it delicious, too." He attacked the beans. "Ah, just to my taste!"

"Aye, we've done soldiering when Tennessee was even rawer'n she is now. I'll never forget that Indian trying to scalp you, General—Judge—" He stopped. "Faith, I haven't it straight. You said you're a militiaman again, sir?"

Lee spoke up while Jackson vigorously munched his beans. "Sir, will you tell us about our war with the British?"

General Jackson shot him a look. "I will. And a greater tale of fuddy-duddying in Washington, ye'll never hear! For though we snatched our independence from George the Third back in '76, we may again find ourselves under Britain's thumb unless President Madison and those stump-heads around him soon come to their senses!"

He ate some more beans, then gestured angrily with his fork. "A year ago, seeing plain what was brewing, I tendered my services to the War Department, and I gave 'em a detailed plan for smashing once and for all British power in Canada. But I'm not Regular Army, and there's resentment at volunteers. And politics and jealousy and personalities clashing. So they gave my plan to others, who've ruined it. And they kept me a-stewing.

"Finally," he continued, "the War Department sent seventy commissions to our Governor Blount. See how the Department still ignores me? But the Governor filled my name in the first commission, making me Major General of United States volunteers. General Wilkinson kept me from taking my troops to New Orleans to help him—why, I don't know. It will be a problem to defend the territory from here to the gulf. 'Tis wild country and full of Indians. And with liquor, money, and promises the scheming Redcoats are setting 'em afire against the United States.

"What I'll do now," he said bitterly, "I know not. Should I, with God's help, succeed in helping my country, I firmly believe my enemies in Washington will be greatly chagrined. Think of that! When our nation's in danger!"

He devoured the last of his beans, declined more, and sipped the steaming acorn brew from his cup.

Lee ventured to speak again. "Sir, I don't understand this war. Why is it?"

General Jackson wiped his chin with the fine linen of Mrs. Baird's napkin. Picking up his clay pipe, he re-lighted it with an ember from the fire.

"A war's so vast, and one man's so tiny, 'tis indeed hard to understand. But in simple 'tis this: Back in 1776 our colonies won their political independence. But Britain's great influence has remained over our shipping and trade. Because of her wealth, d'ye see? Now 'tis an issue: shall we win our economic freedom or forever remain weak?

"Ye see, lad," he explained, "British merchants making large profits can pay large taxes to the Royal Treasury. When our shrewd Yankee traders cut British profits smaller, their Treasury suffers. So Britain wants to smash United States competition."

"I've heard, sir, that the British halt our vessels at sea. They take off American tars and force them to serve the King."

" 'Tis true. On pretense of seeking British deserters, they've stopped near nine hundred of our vessels on the high seas, taken off several thousand good Americans, and impressed 'em into their crews. All because Britain badly needs men, being also at war with Napoleon.

"Well, this crime started our fight. It appears that certain interests in England believe she is now powerful enough to wreck our government and take us back as vassal colonies."

"We're Fighting a Fool's War!"

"So that's why we are at war," Mr. Baird mused.

"But, sir," Lee asked, "is there not land fighting too?"

"Yes, there's land fighting too. For the British plan is to crush us." Using the ember with which he had lighted his pipe, General Jackson drew a rough map on the earthen floor. "Look, lad. And you, Adam—you know a bit of military strategy.

"Let this picture our continent. Here," he said, indicating, "is the St. Lawrence River flowing to the ocean across our north border from the Great Lakes. Here is the Mississippi, flowing from the Lakes a thousand miles to the Gulf. Now Quebec, at the mouth of the St. Lawrence, is the supply port for all Canada. The British gathered an army there. And they expect friendly Indians scattered westward to the Lakes to help them set the whole border afire, cross it, and rend us apart.

"So what's to be done? My plan was to strike quickly and capture Quebec. Then Britishers inland and all their friendly Indians couldn't get supplies. I'd also strengthen our fort at Detroit and establish other forts where needed."

General Jackson sighed. "I was ignored. Nothing was done for precious months, and meantime Quebec was amply garrisoned. Finally, using some of my plan, the War Department sent an expedition. It was nine months late, ill-planned and ill-led, hence was routed and destroyed. What a defeat! And Detroit? Surrendered without firing a shot!"

"Then we're losing!" Mr. Baird exclaimed.

"The nation's in grave peril. Our northern campaign has bogged down and the British will try to cut off New England from the rest of our country. They may even land an army to march on Washington. If they capture our capital—" He shook his head. "We're fighting a fool's war, and fools are easily beaten." There was silence save for the snap of a log in the fireplace.

"With slices cut off, a loaf of bread becomes smaller and easier to hold," Lee remarked.

"Hear that, Adam? A wide-awake boy with no military experience sees it instantly. But politics, sectional strife, bickering—" General Jackson dropped on a three-legged stool. "God grant they see it now in Washington—though it may be too late. We may be beaten," he mourned.

Adam Baird stirred. "General, what about our southern border—the Mississippi Territory and New Orleans? I take it the British may also drive at us from the south. You are raising a force to meet that threat?"

"My force of volunteers, which I boated down to Natchez, has been dismissed from service by the War Department. Now the defense of New Orleans is left to that schemer, Wilkinson, as I had to march my men home. I fear for our few forts along the Gulf. The British there too are urging the Indians to rise against us."

He rose as if remembering. "But I cannot linger, friends. I must confer this night at Crawford's Mill, so I have nine miles to ride. I thank you for your hospitality, Adam, and it is good to see my old sergeant again."

"I'll fetch your horse, sir." Lee hurried out.

When he brought the horse around, the General and Adam Baird stopped talking, as if they had been discussing him. The visitor mounted but delayed a moment. "What's your future, Lee?" he inquired.

"Sir, I would like to read law. Of course, I shall need some funds. But do you think there is opportunity in the law, General Jackson?" he added.

"A willing man possessed of a quick mind can have any future he wants, Lee, in this new nation. If it survives," he added darkly. Then he smiled. "I was attorney general of Tennessee Territory at twenty-one. At thirty-one I was Senator of our new State. Then a judge, and now a general. You, perhaps, can do better. The opportunities are too many for a man with only one lifetime."

He leaned, offering his hand, which Lee took quickly. "Your father was the best sergeant who ever served under me," General Jackson told him. "For his sake, if ever I can give you advice or aid of any nature—call on me. My farm, The Hermitage, will always welcome the kin of Adam Baird. Again, thanks for your hospitality. Good-by!"

CHAPTER TWO

DEERHIDE CALLS

Father and son stood watching until the tall, thin figure was gone in the night. As the hoofbeats died away, they turned and went back into the cabin. It seemed that neither felt like talk for a few moments, and Adam Baird busied himself unlacing and tugging off his heavy boots while Lee washed and put the supper dishes away.

His father sat smoking his pipe and staring at the fire. Lee sat down on the stool General Jackson had occupied. After a moment their glances met.

"That's the man I've oft talked about, lad. He's a born leader," his father said.

"Indeed, there is something compelling about him that I can't describe. When he speaks you feel 'tis a carefully-weighed opinion and 'tis right. I think he would make a fierce enemy," Lee added.

"Aye. He's hot-tempered, too. But he means to be just. And when he commands men, there's no hardship they suffer that he won't share. He fears nothing that walks this earth. And he has a simple man's faith in Divine Providence."

They did not speak while a minute passed. Refilling his pipe, Mr. Baird caught Lee's eyes. "Are ye sure ye want to read law and become a lawyer?"

"Quite sure. Mother taught me reading and writing and ciphering, so I am perhaps not too ignorant. Faith, I've already more learning than most boys I've met. But—" Lee shrugged. We lack funds, and we have this farm. It takes two to work it."

His father puffed on his pipe, thinking. "Our country's at war, lad. I'm an old soldier. I can drill men and lead 'em, too. And my old militia chief's been called back to service." He studied his pipe. "We own some produce safe in Nashville. A lad, if he got permission to read law with some solicitor, could get along, perhaps."

"Do you mean, Father—"

"Aye. General Jackson needs volunteers. I'd have spoken up when he was here, but you and I are alone in the world and I wanted to talk about it first. Winter's coming on," he reminded. "It's the season for change."

"But the farm?"

"It'll wait."

"But I thought of volunteering too! Shouldn't we both—"

His father's look stopped him. "You're young. One of us should go, and I'm the one. Maybe later, if you're needed enough."

"But if two of us went—"

His father smiled but shook his head, and Lee knew he could not gain permission to enlist. Mr.

Baird rose and tapped out his pipe on the fireplace facing.

"Let's sleep on it. We'll talk more tomorrow."

In silence they got out their blankets and spread them on the floor. Lee banked the fire so that a few coals would remain in the morning to ignite dry logs. When he finished, Adam Baird was already lying blanketed and with his eyes closed. Before Lee had arranged himself, his father was snoring.

In the dim log cabin, with the dying fire sending only an occasional stray tongue of light across the earth floor, Lee lay reviewing General Jackson's visit and thinking what his future might be like.

There was Venus to consider. What would he do with the filly if he left the farm and went, say to Nashville, to study law? The thought of selling her made rebellion rise in him. No, he couldn't! Yet, reading law without pay in some solicitor's office, he could not afford to stable her.

He could sell her to General Jackson, of course. If ever he sold her, it would be best to do so to General Jackson, who would surely give Venus the best of care on his great estate.

But Lee did not want to sell her. He could not bear to think of it!

As for studying law—he really did want that. He had done farm work without complaint ever since they had come here three years ago. But he had never liked it. He had liked better working in the general store his father had previously operated a hundred miles to the east, in the village of Water-gap. In the store there had always been people to talk with and things to talk about and to learn. But here, chopping down trees, then tediously hewing out the stumps to make more land for the plow—it had been dull and silent and lonely.

Perhaps General Jackson would recommend him to a firm of attorneys in Nashville. How long must a man read law before he could take the examination? Once he became an attorney, Lee could have his own office in which to consult with clients. Perhaps he might some day become a judge! Yes, he would like that, and—

Still thinking about it, he must have drifted asleep. Then something—a sound, a slight movement—brought him bolt upright.

For an instant the inky dark of the log cabin told him nothing. The fire was hidden in ashes. Gradually Lee sensed that his father no longer lay there.

Frowning, he reached over and felt of the empty blankets. He cocked his head, puzzled, and listened. Still he heard nothing. Yet alarm started in his stomach and ballooned within him, sending the warm blood faster through his veins.

Noiselessly, Lee rose. Going to the fireplace, he reached above it to feel for the deer rifle that always hung there. His eyes narrowed as he discovered it was gone.

Had his father silently departed to join General Jackson? But no, there seemed no likelihood, no reason, for that. Then—

Outside there was a shot.

Lee gulped. In a trice he was snatching for his boots and hurriedly jerking them on. He heard a muffled cry—then another shot. The first had been his father's deer rifle: he knew its report well. The second, less loud, might have been from a pistol.

He had his keen-edged hunting knife in his fist as he darted for the door. Bushwhackers, of course! They had come to—

The door opened against his hand outstretched for its thonged handle. Swiftly Lee shrank back, letting it swing against his chest as it went wide. A man, only vaguely seen, entered a few steps. In his right fist he had some weapon; his left hand was on the door-edge.

Lee sprang. His intent was to leap on the man from the side, at the same time driving his knife into the fellow's back. For it was not his father—of that he was certain. So it must be one of the scoundrels General Jackson had warned of, and all bushwhackers were cold-blooded killers. A man had best strike first!

But some instinct had told the prowler of his presence, and the fellow stepped away and turned as Lee sprang. They met chest-to-chest, and Lee's knife drove over the fellow's shoulder without harming him.

Lee felt something hard jammed between them. Its heavy feel told him it was a pistol. He drove a fist at the bristly countenance close to his while at the same time he pulled back his knife. They fell apart—and the pistol exploded.

The blaze of burning powder gave Lee a glimpse of a jowled, bearded face stamped with evil. There was a tug at Lee's biceps, then a stab of pain, so that he knew he had been hit—but not seriously. A little blinded by the flash, he was instantly twice as furious, and slashed viciously with his knife.

It brought a gasp. The other fell back. His pistol useless, he would be drawing his own knife now from his boot. Lee rushed him, somehow balancing to kick at the fellow's right leg where the knife would be, and at the same time stabbing hard again at his torso.

He connected, too—but felt a new thrill of fear at the man's choked-out: "Deerhide!"

Lee whipped back. A big form blocked the doorway. It rushed in, and another man appeared. Three men in the dark room were pitted against Lee.

It would be foolhardy to remain while there was any chance of escape. His first impulse was to try darting through the door. But the second newcomer paused there, and even if he could be dislodged, suppose a confederate was close behind him?

His decision instantly made, Lee dodged the

blade that hissed through the air close to his face. He whirled and darted toward the cabin's only window. His mother had insisted on having that window to let out smoke when the chimney refused to draw well on damp mornings. It had cost much extra work of cutting logs and fitting them, but Mrs. Baird had got her way. And later, Lee had carefully smeared bear grease over two copies of the Nashville newspaper, called the *Whig*, and secured them in the opening to let light through.

He was thankful now for his mother's whim! The window was almost chest-high but it was large—and most important, it offered the only way out. Rushing at it, Lee had to estimate its height and nearness in pitch dark; but he gave a terrific leap, held his arms protectively over his head, and breathed a swift prayer.

He went through and outside, though one knee bumped on the window ledge. That spoiled his plan of putting his head down and landing on his shoulders to roll over and leap up at once. It pitched him off-balance, so that he struck on one shoulder with a hard jar and slid several feet.

For an instant he lay helpless, the wind clubbed from his chest. When he did grope onto his knees, pain stabbed through one. But he gained his feet and, choking back his panting, listened.

His eyes glinted. The trio in there had not yet discovered he was gone! Yes . . . now they had.

"—leaped out, you fools!" someone roared. "Git outside! Carve his liver!"

Lee looked quickly this way and that. Turning, he ran for the stable, wondering where his father was and how he could help him. He rounded the rear corner of the cabin and was about to rush into the open side of the barn when something moving caught his eyes. He hesitated. There came a weak gasp from a man in agony.

A lead ball formed in Lee's chest. For an instant he could not move. Then he strode to the deep shadow of the barn wall and knelt. "Father!"

It was Adam Baird lying there on his chest. He clawed the ground like a man seeking strength to withstand pain. As Lee grasped his shoulder and would have turned him onto his back his father gasped hoarsely:

"No! Lee, I—Deerhide—scoundrels wanted—"

He slumped face-down on the ground. And Lee knew he was dead. He stayed kneeling there. He could not make his mind function.

Adam Baird—*dead!*

A warning clanged in his numbed brain. Turning, he heard the trio of toughs bursting out of the cabin. Lee jerked erect—hesitated. But he could not help his father now.

He ran behind the barn and stood trying to think what he should do next—with thoughts of his father tumbling frantically through his mind—with anxiety for Venus. Had they got her?

Abruptly he flattened himself against the barn wall. Sounds came now at the far end of the structure, and Lee's heart seemed to stop beating as he made out the vague form of still another of the notorious Deerhide's gang—leading a horse that must be Venus.

The fellow had no suspicion of his presence. A hail came from near the house. "Ridley? Where the devil's he gone!" Deerhide fumed.

"Here!" Ridley shouted. "Behind the barn!"

Lee turned his knife in his fist so that its heavy, curved butt was uppermost. He rushed at Ridley and drove the butt at the man's skull as hard as he could. He struck again, and a third time. His left hand gripping Ridley's shoulder felt the fellow sag away as he buckled with a moan. He lay still.

Panting, Lee groped for Venus's reins while he stood listening intently, gauging his chance for flight. He pulled the filly around and hastened with her into darkness away from the barn and away from the cabin.

"Where is he? That pinch-faced—"

"Behind the barn, he said. There ain't a thing around here worth Continental paper!" one of the outlaws growled.

"No, the old fool's taken his produce to town, that's why. Hey, Ridley! The boy's got a hoss," the speaker went on. "Said to be a promisin' critter. If

Ridley ain't found that filly, I'll cut his gizzard—"

Lee heard a snarl. They had discovered Ridley.

Lee estimated he was far enough from the barn so it could not matter too much if he revealed his whereabouts. He halted Venus, tossed the reins over her ears, and vaulted astride. As he settled himself on her back, dismay brought an exclamation from him. For red tongues of flame were licking up the corner of the log house!

Deerhide, furious at finding none of the hides and tobacco loot he expected, had set the cabin afire. The barn was sure to catch from it, and the body of Adam Baird would be cremated.

A lump clogged Lee's throat. Eyes closed, he touched his heels to Venus's belly. The filly broke into a brisk trot, her ears cocked back with the alarm she shared with her master. There were shouts behind them as Deerhide heard his quarry escaping, and a pistol was discharged wildly into the night. But Lee had got away, and no outlaw's horse would be likely to overtake Venus and her master.

He had got away, but Adam Baird had not. Adam Baird would not serve again under his old commander, General Jackson . . . nor work the farm . . . nor see his son read law.

"Durn 'em!" Lee burst out. "I'll kill Deerhide if ever we meet again! I'll kill him! I'll kill him!"

CHAPTER THREE

WAITING FOR THE GENERAL

Nashville, situated on the winding Cumberland River, was the largest settlement Lee had ever seen, its population being estimated at several thousand. He had visited it twice with his father but there had not been time to pause and watch the bustle and hurry of this chief trading center west of the Cumberland Mountains. Now employed in John Roston's livery barn just off Market Street, Lee frequently was sent on errands to various parts of the city and had quickly learned his way about its dusty streets.

The day he came riding into town on Venus the noise and seeming confusion had been frightening. Too, the way people only glanced at him, then hurried on about their affairs, made him feel very unimportant. Loneliness crowded his chest and kept a lump in his throat that Lee could not swallow.

He was alone in the world now. He didn't belong to anyone. True, his mother had two sisters somewhere back in Virginia. But he was not certain where they lived, and it must be two hundred miles to Virginia, through wild country and over mountains. And if he did locate his aunts, would they want him to live with them?

Halting Venus beside a plank sidewalk, Lee sat watching and wondering. Before coming to Nashville he had stopped at the neighboring farm of Obediah Kennedy, and with Mr. Kennedy had returned to the heap of smouldering ashes that had been his home. Mr. Kennedy, searching the ruins, had discovered a few charred bones. The fury in his face intensified as he looked from them to Lee.

Lee couldn't keep his chin from quivering nor the tears from welling into his eyes. For a moment they stood in silence. Then they turned away.

"If only I meet him some time—and recognize him!" Lee choked. "I'll kill Deerhide. I'll kill him just as he murdered my father!"

Mr. Kennedy brushed a sleeve across his eyes. "You do it. And you'll save other folks by gettin' rid of him. The sneakin' scoundrel!"

They rode back to the Kennedy farm. Mr. Kennedy had offered to employ Lee, but for wages he would get only his keep. Of course, he had no money nor any clothes save those he wore.

He did not want farm work; he wanted to read law so that some day he could argue cases in court and earn his living. The longer he kept doing farm work, Lee reflected, the longer it would be before he became a lawyer. So he declined the job, thanked Mr. Kennedy, and set out for Nashville.

But the city seemed cold. It was not interested in

a lanky boy alone in the world. It did not even offer him food, and he was growing hungry. What was he to *do?*

Most of that first day Lee walked Venus through the streets or dropped on the ground, holding her reins and watching Nashville folk move briskly about their business. Below the city, at the riverside, it was called Johnson's Landing. Flatboats, barges, keelboats, and skiffs clustered there, some neglected, others loading bales of cotton and hides for the eight-hundred-mile trip downstream to New Orleans. Still other boats had brought westward-bound settlers with their bawling livestock, wagons, plows and bundles of belongings—strong men, sturdy women, big-eyed children, and crying babies. Some flatboats were disgorging goods tediously hauled from the eastern seaboard, and Lee saw crates of bolt cloth, barrels of whisky, turpentine, furniture and nails.

From the river a brown clay road wound up the rocky bluff that, one man told Lee, was of marble. Terry's warehouse, a long, broad structure, sprawled beside the road. Lee remembered that his father had deposited their produce there; but he lacked any paper with which to claim it and had not yet the courage to seek out Mr. Terry and ask about the goods. Along the ascending path stood cabins of logs, some neatly kept, others neglected. Most were occupied by Negroes who worked as roustabouts on the river or servants in the upper town. A few were the homes of white keelboatmen and pilots.

The main thoroughfare of Nashville was Market Street—dusty in dry weather and a brown gumbo when it rained. Along rough board sidewalks stood stores and barns and taprooms. The gray stone taproom was de Monbruen's (de Monbruen was said to have been the first white man to dwell permanently on the site of Nashville). Many of the stores had wooden awnings built over the sidewalk, and all had rails at the sidewalk-edge to which folk tied their horses and oxen while they shopped.

Lee tied his filly to a railing at the public square, then walked around the big stone courthouse, looking at it. He would have liked to go inside—perhaps court was being held and he was curious to see how that was done. His father had described a courtroom he had visited, but Lee wished he could see one for himself. A little later he stood gazing at the barred windows in the rear of the courthouse that showed jail cells must be there. And near-by was a thick post fixed in the ground that he knew was for securing convicted men while they were publicly whipped.

For a long time he stared at a bearded, dirty miscreant fixed in the public stocks. The fellow's ankles and wrists were locked between heavy planks with holes cut in them. He looked miserably uncomfortable, and Lee was glad it was not he sitting there.

He determined he would never do anything against the law lest he be sentenced to the stocks!

Later he sat on the lawn holding Venus's reins while she cropped weeds. Venus could feed anywhere, but Lee was growing very hungry and could not think how to get a meal. He watched two well-dressed gentlemen talking near-by. One turned and went to a sleek saddle horse and mounted and rode away. The other gentleman, about to start off, noticed Lee. He came nearer. "Your horse, lad?"

Quickly Lee got to his feet. "Yes, sir. Her name's Venus. And she can surely run," he added with a touch of pride.

The gentleman smiled. He examined Venus, then looked again at Lee. His gaze noted his rough clothes. "Waiting for someone, I suppose?"

"Well—no, sir. Just resting."

The gentleman took from his pocket what looked like a letter. "Would you like to earn half a dollar? I want this delivered to a certain man, and when you return with his answer I'll pay you."

Lee thought of the food the half-dollar would buy. "Yes, sir," he said promptly. "I don't know Nashville very well, but I'm sure I could do it, sir."

He listened carefully to the directions the gentleman gave. "You'll find me at the Nashville Inn."

Lee looked puzzled. The gentleman pointed. "That tall building yonder is a hotel, the Nashville Inn. See, there's another, the City Hotel. Don't confuse them. I'll be at the Inn, next door to that cock-pit. Where they hold cock fighting. D'you see it?"

In a moment Lee was astride Venus and on his way. The man to whom he delivered the letter lived in a large several-room log house on a hill not far outside the city. Lee waited while he wrote his reply; as the man handed it to him, he noticed Venus.

"Hm." He walked out to look at the filly. He felt of Venus's chest the way General Jackson had, and carefully examined her legs. "How much do you want for her, lad?"

"Oh," Lee said, surprised, "I can't sell her, sir."

"No? Isn't she yours?"

"Faith, sir, she is. But I just couldn't sell her."

The man looked him over. "I dare say you could use a hundred dollars in cash?"

The sum almost whisked Lee's breath away. He possessed nothing, yet in a matter of minutes he could own a hundred dollars! But it meant not owning Venus any longer, and he could not bear to think of that. "Thank you, sir. I just couldn't sell her. She's all I have."

"Looks a likely bit of horseflesh. She's a runner, or I haven't dealt in horses these last fifteen years. But if she's all you own, I understand," he smiled.

Lee went to mount Venus, then hesitated. "Sir, could you tell me—doesn't General Jackson live somewhere near Nashville? How can I get to see him, sir?"

"I Just Couldn't Sell Her, Sir."

The man's bushy eyebrows raised. "General Jackson? Yes, he lives a few miles farther along this road. He has a large place—six hundred and forty acres. It's called The Hermitage. The house is a big one, and there's a guest house close by, and they're on a hill overlooking the river. Why do you want to see the General?" he added curiously. "Do you know him?"

Lee nodded. "I need to ask him what I should do. I haven't any place to go. And General Jackson told me only a few days since, back on our farm—" He stopped at remembrance of the tragedy there. "He said he would help me if ever I needed help, because my father was his sergeant in the militia."

The short man stood toying with his gold watch chain. "Alas, General Jackson is not at home. I doubt he'll be home for a matter of weeks."

Disappointment showed on Lee's face as, turning, he vaulted astride Venus.

"Just a minute." Stepping nearer, the man looked up at him as if thinking. "I take it, lad, you're in need of lodging and work until you can see the General?"

"Yes, sir, I am," Lee returned earnestly.

The other smiled a little, still toying with his watch chain. "No doubt you know something of horses, and perhaps raised this filly yourself. I own a livery barn in the city," he explained. "I could use a reliable boy there."

Lee's heart bounded. He all but fell off Venus's

back in his eagerness. "I'll work for you, sir! I'll do whatever you require. And I—I love horses, and I can handle them, and usually they like me." He remembered his filly. "Sir, if I could earn food and any sort of lodging at all, and—if I could only keep Venus—" He broke off, watching the man's face eagerly.

The smile had broadened. "I'm John Roston. My livery is just off Market Street, near the Nashville Inn. Anyone can direct you. Yes, you may keep your filly if you like. Of course, I can't afford oats for her."

"No, sir. She won't be in the way. I'll see to that!"

"I'll pay you three dollars a week—or five if you dispose of the filly. You can sleep in the mow. But mind, be very careful of fire!"

A few minutes later, scarcely able to credit his good luck, Lee was trotting Venus back into Nashville to deliver the reply to the gentleman's letter. He found his man, not in the inn, but in the cockpit next door. A lively battle was in progress between two bristling, fierce cocks. But even as Lee entered, one, with a savage lunge, pecked out an eye of the other. The aggressor kept fluttering at his foe and slashing with his spurs until blood began to spatter from the struggling victim. The crowd of men shouted or groaned according to which cock they had wagered on. Abruptly the blinded bird fell, and in an instant the other had furiously hacked him to death.

Delivering the letter, Lee received his half-dollar of pay and at once made his way out of the place. He disliked seeing cocks battle like that, tearing each other to pieces, though it seemed to be a popular enough sport, and many well-dressed gentlemen attended. Even General Jackson, he learned in the next few days, loved cock-fighting and often risked considerable sums on his champion fighter.

Lee spent half his money for food at the public market, then reported to the surly, fat foreman of the livery barn. The fellow looked him up and down. "Who told ye to come to work?"

"Mr. John Roston did."

"Humph!" He eyed Venus critically. "Where'd ye steal that filly?"

"I didn't steal her," Lee retorted. "I raised her from a colt. She's mine, and Mr. Roston said I could keep her in the rear yard. And he said I could sleep in the mow."

"Sleep in the mow then! But mind," the foreman barked, "I'll not have ye thievin' oats for that filly. Now get rid of her. Find brushes and start curryin'. We don't sit around here. We work!"

The foreman, named Emil, did little else but sit around, Lee soon discovered. The work was done by Lee and the several colored boys always around the stable. But though Emil was crusty and sour, it was not difficult staying out of his way if the horses were well-kept and the front of the stable was neat.

Mr. Roston's livery was the principal one in Nashville and comprised more than twenty good carriage horses, a dozen saddle horses, and three teams of heavy draft animals. Because of its central location, it did a good rental business to gentlemen staying at the Nashville Inn or City Hotel. Strangers in the city, these men often desired a driver with a hired carriage, hence Lee soon learned his way among the various streets and even out into the countryside. Too, his modest manner and his expertness with horses won him tips that sometimes equalled his week's wages.

He was waiting a little impatiently for General Jackson to return from wherever he was traveling. The General's absence, Lee thought, must have to do with raising the troops he had spoken of. When he came back to The Hermitage, Lee meant to call upon him and ask advice about his future. He would have to do something about the farm produce in Terry's warehouse. And he wanted to learn more about reading law. But that would be after the war, for hearing talk of it everywhere, Lee wanted now to serve in the army.

His father could not serve as he had desired—because of Deerhide and his ruffian accomplices. Every time Lee thought of that name he clenched his fists and vowed again that if ever he met the rascal he would settle him! But with his father gone, he felt he was needed in General Jackson's forces, and meant to enlist at the first opportunity.

Travelers brought word that the war was going badly. One British Army was fighting down into New England and if not halted might isolate Maine, New Hampshire, Massachusetts and near-by states. This would include Boston, the nation's largest city. It would cripple the United States on the seas, for most vessels were built in New England and most crews came from there. With the fleet crippled for men, vessels and supplies, the remainder of the Atlantic coast would be open to easy invasion. Indeed, British men-o'-war guarding numerous transports had already been sighted off Baltimore, as if another of the King's armies was about to land there, as General Jackson had prophesied.

Lee heard the General's name everywhere. His call for more volunteers had already brought almost twenty-five hundred to Nashville. They came in twos, threes, platoons, and even companies. Some of the officers sported white pantaloons and waistcoats but the men were clad in nut-brown homespun trousers and buckskin shirts. They were a lean, hard-looking lot. Major William Lewis, who was Jackson's quartermaster, had them encamped a little away from Johnson's Landing on the river and was striving to provide sufficient fuel, food and shelter while their numbers increased daily.

All of these woodsmen carried rifles. "The General doesn't want smooth-bore muskets," Major Lewis said. "They don't carry straight. They're good enough for regular soldiers, but we frontiersmen know rifles are better."

One morning in September Lee's work was interrupted with a curt order. "Hitch up those bays and drive the black carriage around to the City Hotel. Colonel Thomas Benton wants it." Emil started away. "And I hope," he muttered, "the outfit don't come back splashed with General Jackson's blood!"

"Sir," Lee exclaimed, "is the General returned?"

"Returned? Of course he is. And in Nashville too, I hear."

Lee frowned. "And is Colonel Benton his enemy?"

Emil stopped and turned. "Don't ye know the feud that's between Tom Benton and his brother Jesse, and the General? And over what? Because the General tried to smooth down a duel between Billy Carroll and Lieutenant Littleton Johnston, for which Jesse Benton and the General were to be seconds. A triflin' quarrel between young hotheads, it was. But because the General sought to stop it, tongues've been waggin' and now it's the Bentons against our Andy!"

He strode off. Lee stood staring, trying to understand. He had heard of Colonel Benton and his brother Jesse coming to the City Hotel that morning. Usually they put up at the Nashville Inn, but because that was General Jackson's favorite place they had today gone to the other hostelry.

Feeling apprehension grow in him, Lee quickly hitched the bays and drove the carriage around to the City Hotel. He kept a sharp lookout for the General but failed to sight him. Lee jumped from the carriage, went indoors, and recognized Colonel Benton.

"Sir, I have the carriage you ordered," he said.

Thomas Hart Benton glanced from under heavy brows. He had been talking earnestly with friends and for an instant did not seem to recall ordering a carriage.

"Oh, yes," he said. "Well, wait, lad." He took out a dollar and tossed it to Lee. "If I don't come in an hour, take the rig back to the livery."

There was something in the air. Lee could feel it as he walked out of the hotel. Men cast searching looks up and down the street as they stood talking in low tones. At the hitchrail, rubbing the horses' noses, he kept a vigilant, wondering watch.

Then he glimpsed the tall, slim figure of General Jackson. With two other men he emerged from the Nashville Inn, diagonally across Court House Square. They came nearer, bound for the post office a little down the street from the City Hotel.

Lee watched them. He could have either called to General Jackson or run to meet him, but he felt this was not the moment, while there was danger in the air. His gaze followed the three men until they vanished into the post office.

Then Jesse Benton, younger and shorter in build than his brother, the Colonel, came out of the City Hotel. Nodding to the hail of a friend, he looked up and down the street. As he swished back his coat, Lee saw that he wore two pistols. Scowling, he turned and entered the barroom next to the hotel after crossing a roofed passageway that led back to a porch overlooking the river.

It was only two or three minutes before General Jackson emerged from the post office. Only one companion was with him now. They came toward Lee, and he felt his pulse quicken as he watched. Would the General and the Bentons meet? Perhaps not, since the brothers now were indoors.

Colonel Benton stepped out of the barroom, where he must have spoken with his brother Jesse. He stood in the passageway—and Lee knew he did not yet see General Jackson approaching. Nor had Jackson seen him.

The air became electric. Suddenly the adversaries did discover each other. General Jackson's knuckles went white over the short whip he carried, and without hesitation he changed course straight at Benton, brandishing it.

"Now defend yourself, you insulting rascal!" Lee heard him snap angrily.

CHAPTER FOUR

OLD HICKORY WOUNDED

Colonel Benton snarled something and swept back the skirt of his coat, reaching for his pistol. Before he could draw it General Jackson had shifted the whip to his other hand and snatched out his own pistol.

"Don't try that, Tom!"

His weapon seemed to be pressing the other's chest. Colonel Benton's face paled and he stood statue-like. General Jackson's icy tones carried to Lee, tensely watching while he held the bridles of the carriage horses.

"This is all foolishness, Tom. There's no honor been blemished, as you ought to know as well as I. But we'll not discuss it on the street. Back up!"

He meant, Lee knew, to get out of view of the fascinated onlookers. At the pressure of the pistol against his chest, Colonel Benton slowly retreated, backing deeper in the passageway. Evidently the General wanted to talk over their dispute on the porch where the curious could not see or hear. Two steps they went, three, four, five . . .

Lee's heart went cold. He strove to cry out. But his voice would not come. Behind General Jackson,

Jesse Benton had stepped out of a doorway from the barroom. Instantly he grasped the situation, and Lee knew that Colonel Benton, gazing over Jackson's shoulder, had spied rescue coming from his brother.

As Jesse Benton drew a pistol, Lee did manage to start a warning. "General—!"

He got no farther before Jesse deliberately fired at Jackson's back. It was a murderous thing to do. Although Lee had plainly seen Jesse's advantage, he had been certain that no gentleman would coldly cut down another who was not even facing him. Lee had expected that Jesse Benton would only call on the General to drop his weapon, and in that way to free the Colonel and take Jackson captive.

But he had fired—with terrible effect. Struck in the back, Jackson staggered violently. The pressure of his trigger finger must have been involuntary. His weapon exploded, and Colonel Benton lurched back as if hit. But as he swayed he was drawing his pistols, and next instant fired them both.

General Jackson pitched heavily to the floor of the passageway. James Sitler, one of the men on the sidewalk rushed at the trio, shouting. As he ran, over his shoulder Lee saw Jesse Benton close in on General Jackson and aim his still-loaded second pistol down at the helpless man.

Before he could fire, James Sitler struck up his arm. Sitler then dropped on one knee beside General Jackson, from whose side a red pool was rapidly spreading out over the flooring. Meanwhile, John Coffee, who had been the General's companion and had watched from the sidewalk—certainly expecting no foul play—was rushing at the combatants. He fired through the mushrooming powder smoke at Colonel Benton. Evidently he missed, but plunged on, clubbing at Jesse Benton as he passed and leaping over the General to charge Colonel Benton.

Impulse prompted Lee also to rush to the General's assistance. But the cries of the men on the sidewalk, the loud reports of the pistols, and the very excitement in the air made the team of bays rear up, snorting, wild-eyed, their forefeet slashing out. Lee almost lost hold of their bridles. But he hung on somehow, facing the frightened horses and arching his body away from their slashing hoofs which drove so close they tore his homespun shirt.

By the time he got them a little quieted, the fray had ended. Mr. Coffee, Lee learned later, had caused Colonel Benton to retreat to the head of a stairway from the porch, where he suddenly had lost his footing and toppled backward an entire flight.

Mr. Stockley Hays, another partisan of General Jackson's, had followed Mr. Coffee to the rescue, whipping the sword out of his sword-cane as he charged. He would have run Jesse Benton through with it, too, but the point caught on a button of young Benton's coat and the blade snapped. Jesse drew still another loaded pistol, thrust it against Mr. Hays's body, and pulled the trigger—but the charge failed to explode. Whirling, Jesse bolted into the barroom and made his escape.

A crowd collected. Lee, getting his team quiet enough to tie to the hitchrail, burned with anxiety to be of some aid. He feared General Jackson was dead—as indeed did every other man who had witnessed the shooting. He darted under the hitchrail and wormed his way through the crowd, careless of whom he gouged with his elbows or upset.

He halted in the front rank. A wave of weakness went over him at sight of General Jackson lying on his side while blood oozed steadily through his torn coat and from the wound in his left shoulder.

"Is there a surgeon?" Mr. Hays called.

Men exchanged looks. Apparently there was none in the crowd. "I'll fetch Doctor Linester!" someone cried, and thrust his way free.

Mr. Hays sought to ease the General, who lay limp and ashen-faced but who seemed to be conscious. Lee stepped forward with a quick suggestion. "Sir, I have a carriage at the sidewalk. Can't we take him to his hotel?"

Mr. Hays's face proved that this suggestion was considered a good one. There was quick talk among the men.

"We'll have to lift him carefully!"

"Let's get him on a bed!"

"The surgeon can care for him better if we—"

"General," Mr. Hays questioned anxiously, "can you stand to be moved?"

The gray eyes, not so sharp now as usual, looked up at him steadily and seemed to give assent. "Two of you help here!" As two men promptly stepped forward, Mr. Hays grasped the General's ankles. "One hold him from underneath. We must carry him flat as possible. Ready?"

Lee turned. "Clear the way! One side, gentlemen!"

The onlookers fell back to the public sidewalk and there dispersed to give ample space. Lee jerked loose the rope halter at the hitchrail and grabbed the bays' bridles as he had a few moments since. He held them rooted to the spot despite their nervous flaring of nostrils and uneasy shifting of feet as they sniffed the odor of blood.

"To the Nashville Inn, sir?" he asked of Mr. Hays.

The men were gently lifting General Jackson into the carriage. He was so tall that his legs dangled over one side; but his injured back and his head were flat on the seat cushion. Mr. Hays remained on his knees on the floor, holding the General firmly as he caught Lee's eyes and nodded.

"Thank you, gentlemen. If you wish, you could be at the Inn when we arrive, and help carry him to his room."

"Clear the Way," Lee Shouted

The two helpers nodded and quickly set off across Court House Square. As Lee tugged the team forward at a walk, Mr. Coffee appeared from the passageway. His face showed rage he could not express in words and he looked rather the worse for a fierce tussle. He strode out brushing his coat and anxiously eyeing the carriage.

At a quick, steady walk Lee led the team to the corner, turned it, and headed for the Nashville Inn. By the time the equipage halted there, the two volunteers were waiting and had apprised the manager of General Jackson's injuries. Two husky colored men stood by to help carry the General and the doors were held wide by two others while the manager stood near giving orders.

As the General was carried inside and up the wide staircase, Lee found himself trembling. Anxiety kept quivering through him lest General Jackson, his only friend in Nashville, die. For his wounds were serious —no doubt of that!

He stood stroking the bays' muzzles and trying to be calm himself. Then he climbed into the carriage and for an instant stood staring at the bloody seat cushion and floor. Swallowing hard, he twitched the reins and started the bays back for the livery barn.

He had no apprehension of a scolding from the fat Emil for the bloody equipage—and indeed, none came. Seated smoking in the stable doorway, Emil spied the blood at once and opened his mouth for snarling protest. But swiftly Lee explained.

"General Jackson's been shot. They've killed him!"

Emil sensed the grief in Lee's voice and looks. "What!" he bellowed. "They've killed him? General Jackson! What tarnation fools'd do that? They can't —they *can't!*" he roared. Lunging from his chair, he grasped Lee's shoulder and shook him.

"Who did it? Who killed General Jackson?"

"The B-Bentons. Oh," Lee shuddered, "that cowardly Jesse Benton! I'm fearful they've killed him, Emil. He bleeds so! We took him to the Inn, and they're calling doctors for him now. I—I couldn't help getting the carriage bloody, because—"

"Help? Bloody? If ye'd come back here without assisting Andy Jackson, I'd cut ye to ribbons! Who cares about cushions? So they've hurt him? They've hurt him!" He halted, struck by a thought. "But ye say he ain't dead yet?"

"No. Though he's badly hurt, Emil."

"Well—" The usually surly stable foreman stood with eyes lowered. Grimly he said: "He ain't easy to kill. Not Old Hickory. He's tough—frontier-tough. And if any man can live through what he got—" He squinted. "Then he'll live through't, that's all. I pray he will!"

He called colored boys to unhitch the horses and gave them orders to wash out the seat cushion in cold water. Then he made Lee recount the whole episode in its full details.

When Lee finished Emil sat in his chair again, biting on the stem of his pipe. He looked up. "Why are you so concerned? You don't even know him."

"But I do, Emil. He and my father were close friends. General Jackson is the only—well, the only friend I have. I've been waiting for weeks to ask his advice what I should do."

Emil did not probe into Lee's reason for wanting advice. He only studied him a moment, his manner kindlier than Lee had ever known it. He seemed to decide something. "All right, boy. I see you're all bound up in the General's welfare. And so's every sane man who appreciates greatness. So you go and try to learn what's brewin' at the Nashville Inn. Come back now and again and keep me informed. And Mr. John Roston'll want to know when he comes down. Be off with ye!"

Lee hurriedly departed. The street before the Inn was packed with people anxiously awaiting word of the General's condition. But even as Lee approached, someone haranguing the crowd shouted and pointed toward the City Hotel.

"—go and get 'em, I say! And if General Jackson dies—"

"They hang!" someone shouted.

"Aye! *They hang!*" The crowd took it up.

Almost as one man they turned and started grimly flooding across the square toward the City Hotel in search of the Bentons.

Lee waited for them to clear away. Then he entered the Nashville Inn and stood listening to the angry talk of the few men there.

"—every surgeon in town," someone said.

"—wish someone would come and tell us! He's a hard-built man, but no one can withstand the loss of too much blood."

"The General's in command of the whole defense of this part of the country—clear to the Gulf," another man reminded. "Who else is fit for the post? And with the Indians likely to rise any instant!"

"The way those dunderheads in Washington run the war," still another gentleman growled, "they'll lose it before Andy Jackson has a chance to prove what he can do!"

Lee moved from knot to knot of the excited, anxious men. At last a step was heard on the stairs. All heads turned, and Lee recognized young Mr. Stockley Hays descending. He was white-faced and tired-looking and disheveled, and there were dark stains of blood on the sleeves of his coat.

He stopped. The throng in the Inn waited.

"The doctors," he said quietly, "desire to amputate General Jackson's arm. We have every doctor in town here, and they all agree it should be done. But General Jackson regained consciousness and was told, and he—" Mr. Hays's worry was plain in his pause. "The General thought it over a moment.

Then he said, 'I'll keep my arm, gentlemen!'"

There was a rustle through the crowd. Mr. Hays came on down the stairs to confer with the manager. They spoke in low tones; then Mr. Hays again faced the waiting men. "Gentlemen, I know you will understand. It is very important that there be nothing, not the slightest noise, to disturb General Jackson."

Quickly the crowd comprehended the suggestion. Men looked at each other, then in silence began to move out of the hotel lobby.

Lee delayed. Then he decided also to go, and was almost to the door when Mr. Hays, staring at him curiously, called out, "Boy!"

Lee halted. Mr. Hays came across to him. "Aren't you the lad who offered the carriage?"

"Yes, sir. I—I hope the General will get well!"

Mr. Hays put a hand on his shoulder. "So do we all, lad. Your name?"

"Lee Baird, sir. General Jackson is my only friend in Nashville. I've been waiting weeks for his return to ask his advice on a—a matter."

"I see." Mr. Hays hesitated. "I doubt you'll ever get to confer with him. The General may not live."

Lee turned away as Mr. Hays did. They walked apart, the one for the staircase leading upward to General Jackson's room, the other out the door to report to Emil that there was grave doubt General Jackson would be alive on the morrow.

CHAPTER FIVE

NEWS FROM FORT MIMS

On the following day the General's condition was reported still poor and doubt persisted that with his considerable loss of blood he could live. But at least, as Mr. Roston said at the livery barn, the most critical first hours were past. If the patient could avoid blood poisoning and pneumonia and gradually win his strength back over a long convalescence, he should eventually get well.

Nashville anxiously awaited bulletins on the General's condition for several days. Even his enemies, Mr. Roston said, wanted him to get well, for every man respected the owner of The Hermitage farm for his oft-demonstrated patriotism and for his genius in leadership.

The Bentons, who evidently had come to Nashville on some business or other, remained at the City Hotel several days. Their stay could not have been pleasant for they were the focus of glares and muttered threats wherever they went. Wisely, they departed before long.

After a week the General was removed to The Hermitage. It fell to Mr. Roston to supply a carriage, and Lee asked to be its driver. Mr. Hays was first to recognize him as several men carried General Jackson downstairs and out to the carriage and gently placed him in it.

When the equipage got under way, Mr. Hays leaned from the back seat. "How are you today, lad? You see our patient much improved, wouldn't you say?"

Lee had shuddered at sight of the patient, for his face was chalky and his cheeks sunken and he looked more eagle-like than ever, though a fragile eagle now. At the question, however, he managed a smile and a nod. "Yes, sir, he looks ever so much better. I doubt not he'll feel better, too, once he's home again."

He drove very carefully, avoiding jolts and bumps as much as possible. The gentlemen carried on desultory talk and as Lee turned off the highway into The Hermitage grounds, slowing the team to a walk, Mr. Hays leaned forward again.

"General Jackson studied you quite a while, lad, and he knows you now. He asks what you are doing here? He saw you on a farm last, he says."

Lee nodded. "My father is no more, sir. That bushwhacker, Deerhide, attacked us in the night and killed him. When the General is better," he added, "I would value highly a brief talk with him."

Mr. Hays relayed this and leaned forward again with a message. "He says you may come to see him a week hence, Lee. He'll want a talk with you. Can you be here?"

Indeed he could and would be here! Lee had a slight nod and thin smile from the patient as ready hands lifted him from the carriage in front of the big manor house that was General Jackson's home. That nod and smile relieved Lee's worry, for he felt suddenly that his father's old commander would get well. He was determined to do so, and he was a man of powerful will.

Mrs. Jackson, a small lady with black hair and quick eyes, thanked Lee before, worriedly, she turned and followed her husband into the house. Later, when he drove Mr. Hays back to Nashville, Lee felt it was going to be a long convalescence, no doubt of that; but he knew the General would get well.

On the following Thursday he rode again to The Hermitage, this time on Venus. She had not had enough exercise of late and he had no heart to prevent her from a good run. But he had not counted on being unable to stop her and whirled up the drive at full gallop before he could pull her in at the front porch steps.

He slid off her back and rubbed her muzzle after he had tied her to a railing. "You're nothing but a racer, are you?" Lee grinned. "I'll wager you might even beat—"

"Could she beat my Truxton?" a voice called.

Lee turned and discovered General Jackson in an

easy chair on the porch. A heavy rug was over his legs and he wore an overcoat and cap. He was sitting out for the sunshine and fresh air.

Lee mounted the steps as the General beckoned. "I don't know if she could beat Truxton, sir," he said, taking off his cap.

"Sit there, lad. But ye think your filly could. Eh?"

Lee's grin widened. "Yes, sir, I think she might."

"Well, perhaps we can try 'em some day. You've a fast horse there, no doubt of that. How much'll ye sell her for?"

Lee shook his head. "I couldn't sell her. Do you think," he ventured boldly, "we really could hold a race, General?"

The sharp eyes sparkled. "Perhaps. But not till I can attend. And you'd want to ride your filly, I suppose." One thin hand gestured Lee to a chair. "We'll keep it in mind. Mr. Hays tells me that your father was foully slain the very night I visited you. I didn't know that. And I'm sorry!"

"Yes, sir, he was." Lee studied his hands. "And if ever I can find that Deerhide, I shall slay him, and quickly."

"He was furious because you hadn't any produce for him to steal, eh? But he's always quick to kill, anyway. The trouble is," General Jackson went on, "nobody knows who Deerhide is. Would you recognize him if you saw him again?"

"I'm not sure that I would. I glimpsed a whiskery face, rather full and round and I've seen many a man like that. But I hope somehow to identify him. And then—" Lee stopped.

"I wish we could dispose of that scoundrel. He and his gang are the worst. Though there are some bad 'uns between here and New Orleans, from all accounts. Robbing and pillaging keelboats bound down-river to market.

"What's your future, young Baird?" he queried, after a pause.

Lee looked at him earnestly. "I've seen the troops you're raising, sir, encamped down at the Landing. I'd like to join them."

General Jackson only studied him. "And later?"

"I would like to read law and become an attorney. I read and write and cipher pretty well, and perhaps I could improve in those. You encouraged me, sir, to study law, and 'tis what I've always had in mind."

"I see. There's still your farm, though."

"Yes, sir. But I'm not cut out to keep farming always. And I—I don't want to go back there, sir," he explained.

"No? You want to be a soldier, and later on, to study law and try cases in court? Well, Lee, I won't take you as a soldier."

The abruptness of that startled him. Lee began to rise, but sat down again in his chair. "You won't? But I can shoot well," he protested. "And as my father intended joining you but now cannot–"

"No," General Jackson said, "I won't take you. We've all the men we can supply, and you are quite young. Later, if there's need, you can soldier. But I advise you not to do it yet.

"Your father," he went on, "had some property in Terry's warehouse, didn't he? Is it still there?"

"I think it is. I have no paper of any kind to claim it. And I wouldn't know what to do with it. So I waited about that, sir, until I could ask your advice what I should do."

General Jackson leaned back in his chair. He matched the tips of his long, bony fingers as he stared out over the Cumberland glinting in the sunshine below the hill.

"Well, now, you seem to be a bright enough lad. And your father did say you've got your heart set on the law. Don't go to soldiering yet, though you may be needed later. Get started reading law as soon as possible. That would be best. Do you have money?"

Lee shook his head. "Only what I earn at Mr. Roston's livery barn."

"But you own your father's goods in Terry's warehouse. Why not sell that, and support yourself on it while you read with a good firm of attorneys?"

Lee sat forward. "Yes, sir. But–how do I sell it? How do I get hands on it first?"

"I'll write a note to Mr. Terry saying I knew your

father and I know you, and it's safe for him to release the goods to you. As for selling it—you could get a pittance here in Nashville. But you could get far more if you take your hides and cotton and tobacco to New Orleans. That's where prices are high. So why not go there?"

Lee, with eyes shining, waited.

"It's a dangerous trip, and a rough one. But I think you could manage it. You wouldn't require more than a small part of a good-sized keelboat. It happens I'm sending some goods downstream shortly now." He gazed at Lee. "Would you like to go with that shipment? It'll be a cluster of boats carrying produce for many folk around here. Your services will pay your freight charges. With the war and all, there aren't many men available, which is to your advantage. I think the experience would be good."

"I'll go, sir! Although—" He frowned. "'Twould delay my studies."

"Yes, perhaps by several months. But you have time; don't be impatient, lad. First things must be put first. Now," he said, "it's settled that you're willing to go. Where'll you sell your goods in New Orleans?"

Lee's doubtful expression was sufficient answer. The General smiled. "Sell to the man who offers you most. They're hungry for our produce down there, lad. New Orleans is the great market for all we can grow here in Tennessee. That's why," he reflected grimly, "the British are going to try to seize New Orleans from us, sooner or later. It would be a serious blow to our nation if they succeeded."

The General seemed lost in thought for a moment; then he turned to Lee once more. "You sell your produce, and you bring the money back to Nashville. This is a good city to settle in, at least until you like some other better. Now, the trip home is as dangerous as that downstream. There are men who'll follow you from New Orleans and waylay you if they can. There are plenty of thieves in the world," he sighed.

"I believe I could make it, sir. Then I'm to return here and—?"

"I'll see that you get to read law with a good firm. Perhaps it'll be Burgess, Nielsen and Pierce. I'll speak to them about you before I go away. What about your filly? Now don't you want to sell her? You can't take her keelboating, you know, and she wouldn't help you any in New Orleans, if you could."

Lee gazed at Venus quietly cropping grass in the yard. "I hate to think of leaving her," he said slowly. "And faith, I don't know where I can leave her. But I won't sell her," he added firmly.

General Jackson pursed his lips as if to hide another amused look. "Leave her here. I've acreage enough, and she'll be safe. Maybe," he suggested with a twinkle in his gray eyes, "we'll arrange that race some day. Who knows?"

Lee's heart bounded. "Thank you, General Jackson. And I couldn't leave Venus anywhere else I'd feel so sure of."

They heard the sound of hoofbeats, gradually coming nearer. General Jackson stared toward the dusty highway that lay beyond a copse of trees. Lee also watched and suddenly saw a rider leaning low over his horse's whipping mane as the pair came thundering up the road toward the house.

Lee jumped to his feet and ran down to grasp the reins the soldier in faded blue uniform flung to him as he threw himself off the horse. The man ran up the porch steps, halted, saluting, and offered a packet of papers. "For you, General Jackson!"

Lee, only a few yards away, could see and hear all. He watched the General rip the seals of the packet and open the letter it contained. As he did so, Mrs. Jackson appeared in the doorway, having heard the galloping horse. Behind her was Major William Lewis, the General's quartermaster, and with them Lieutenant Littleton Johnston, who was aide to the General.

They came out on the porch. The soldier stood stiffly at attention until General Jackson's gesture let him assume an easier position. "Take a chair, Rachel," he said tenderly to Mrs. Jackson.

He read the letter swiftly. His eyes became very

stern, and his whole thin face seemed to harden. He looked up at the expectant faces. "The Creek Indians have risen. They have massacred some two hundred and fifty persons at Fort Mims, in Mississippi Territory."

"The Creeks? At Fort Mims?" Mrs. Jackson echoed. "Andrew, is that not the region some folk call Alabama? Far to the south of here?"

"It is, my dear."

"The Creek Indians have risen—with the urging of British liquor and British gold!" Major Lewis exclaimed.

"Let us hope the Cherokees and Choctaws remain peaceable!" Lieutenant Johnston said.

General Jackson nodded. His mouth was but a thin slash in the lower part of his face. He noticed the dispatch rider, however, and, summoning Ned, an elderly Negro, asked him to make the man comfortable and give him food. When the soldier had gone, the General sat tapping the letter on the back of one hand.

"Coffee's cavalry can get there soonest," Major Lewis said.

"It is unfortunate, General, that you are in poor health," Lieutenant Johnston said.

Mrs. Jackson leaned and put her hand on her husband's arm. "Now you will be very restless and worried," she said regretfully. "You won't be a good patient now, Andrew."

His look at her was affectionate even though his face kept that rock-like sternness. He glanced at his aides.

"Gentlemen, you are right and you are wrong. You are right in saying that Colonel Coffee and his cavalry can get there soonest. We will send him at once. But it is a long, hard way to Fort Mims, and the damage there has already been done. And more, doubtless, will be done before our force can arrive so far south.

"You are wrong," he went on, "in thinking Colonel Coffee's will be our only troops to go. For this is but the first of many attacks. I have been expecting an outbreak but I knew not where. The British have fired their first gun of the campaign, and it will be a long campaign and a very hard one. But we have no choice save to meet them on their own terms—though perhaps," he said dryly, "with a little more experience in frontier fighting methods.

"Lieutenant Johnston, your pen and paper at once."

Lieutenant Johnston strode into the house for his writing materials. General Jackson and his wife held each other's eyes a long moment. "But you can't go, Andrew!" she protested. "You aren't fit to travel. You aren't well!"

He reached for her hand and held it. "The campaign has opened," he said again. "Eh, Lee?" he called, noticing him over the porch rail.

"Yes, sir. Now can I join your militia? Because, sir, I—"

"No. You may not." The General almost smiled at Lee's impetuousness. "You have your orders to remain a civilian for the time being. It is best and you will be proving yourself a useful citizen. Later, mayhap, I shall need you."

"Rachel," he said in a gentler tone, "I have a duty."

He looked at her, and Lee knew she would not protest further because it would be useless. The General glanced at Major Lewis. "The health of your general is restored, Billy. We march in nine days."

"But, sir! You can't be well enough—" Major Lewis stopped. He knew too well there was no gainsaying what Andrew Jackson willed. He knew, as Mrs. Jackson knew, that the General somehow would have himself well enough at least to start the long, arduous trek over the wild country of the Mississippi Territory. Hence it was useless to argue or protest. Because General Jackson would be going with his troops nine days from now—not eight days, not ten days, but nine days—rain or shine, snow or sleet—afoot or horseback. He would be going.

Lee, listening raptly to this granite man, this greatest soldier of Tennessee, almost jumped when, a few minutes later, his name was again spoken. He hurried up onto the porch and took the two letters

Major Lewis Protested in Vain

which Lieutenant Johnston had written at General Jackson's dictation.

"One, lad, is to Mr. Terry. He will help you load your produce on the keelboat of mine named there. The other letter introduces you to Rob Rawlins, whom folk call Red Feather Rawlins. He is my agent and in charge of taking my produce down to New Orleans. You are to accompany him. Do you understand?"

"Yes, sir, I do. And thank you very much!"

A gesture waved that aside. "The craft start down-river day after tomorrow, so you have not much time. Leave your filly in Mr. Roston's livery and one of my boys will get her tomorrow sundown and bring her here. Don't worry about her, Lee. She'll be well cared for and frequently exercised. Of course, one of my boys will ride her—you don't object to that?"

"No, sir. You are very generous, General Jackson."

The other gave a slow wink. "I'm selfish. But don't tell it abroad, eh? Now, lad—" He extended his hand. "We mayn't meet for many months—if God let's us meet ever. You're sure you can guard your property, and sell it, and get the money back here safely? If I've not returned, present yourself to the law firm of Burgess, Nielsen and Pierce, and explain who you are and that I spoke of you. It will be all right, I think. And take earnest care of your funds!"

he warned again.

Lee shook the bony, powerful hand. "I'll look sharp, sir. My father said you were a friend who lasted forever, General Jackson," he added with emotion clogging his throat. "He was very right, indeed he was!"

Their eyes met. "I expect you to turn out a *good* lawyer—mind that. Now begone, Lee. And good luck!"

Lee went down the steps tucking the letters inside his shirt. He wondered if he would ever meet General Jackson again—for it would be a long gruelling, dangerous campaign in Mississippi Territory. And Andrew Jackson was no behind-the-lines general. He would be in the thick of the fighting.

Leaping astride Venus, he touched her with his heels and she shot away from The Hermitage in a fast trot. Lee looked back just before the copse of the trees shut out his view. He waved—and saw Rachel Jackson's handkerchief fluttering, and the General waving.

They were out of sight now. But Lee hoped they would meet again. He wanted to know General Jackson more. He wanted to become as much respected as the older man was. And though that was a great deal to ask, still he could try.

CHAPTER SIX

TRIP ARRANGEMENTS

Having permission to be away from the livery barn all afternoon in return for working late that evening, Lee set about arranging his affairs to leave Nashville. General Jackson had said his agent, Red Feather Rawlins, planned to begin the long down-river trip day after tomorrow, so there was no time to waste. It would be necessary to consult Rawlins about the trip and Mr. Terry concerning Lee's goods in the warehouse.

He had forgotten to ask General Jackson where Rawlins was to be found; however, he thought the man probably would be somewhere along the river front. He went first to the long, low warehouse Mr. Terry owned and asked for the proprietor. The guard pacing up and down with rifle shouldered, paused, looked Lee over carefully, asked what he wanted, then jerked his thumb at a doorway. Entering it, Lee found himself in a crude office where four or five business men sat waiting, and joined them.

From their talk he learned that Mr. Terry had been forced to hire armed guards to protect his property since the militia encampment had come into being less than a mile away.

"Some of those backwoodsmen get drinkin' and unmanageable," one man said to another. "They tried three times to break in here. There's always a lot of riffraff in a body of men like that."

"It's monotonous waiting for action, I suppose. They want excitement," his friend said.

"Well, I wish the lot of 'em would clear out. They don't bring much business to merchants. There's more crime than usual. A lot of loafers they are—just loafers. As for action," he added, "they'll never see any. I'm blest if I know why they were called together. Where's the war?"

"It isn't close to us here in Nashville," the other admitted, "but the country's at war, all right. There's fighting in New England and at sea and—"

"New England? A thousand and more miles! How does that affect us? Are you being hurt?"

"The British may attack us along the Gulf," his friend maintained. "They may set the Indians on the warpath. General Jackson thinks they will. And suppose they should capture New Orleans? Then where would Tennessee sell her produce?"

"Indians! They're hundreds of miles from here. They may kill a few settlers, but what's that to do with Nashville? People know they're taking risks when they go into that wild country. As for New Orleans," the first man continued, "if the British own it, won't they want to buy our goods? No," he ended flatly, "I call it foolishness to keep men under arms to fight an enemy we can't even see—an enemy that won't bother with such wild country as Mississippi Territory, doesn't even want it!"

Lee opened his mouth—then closed it. He had been about to tell the men that Fort Mims had been attacked and its occupants massacred. But it was not his right, really, to spread that news. Possibly General Jackson might not want it known at once. If he did, he could announce it himself.

The talk ended when one of the men was called in Mr. Terry's office. For an hour Lee awaited his turn. When it came, he found a short, wiry, restless man behind a fine mahogany desk which must have been brought from the East at considerable expense. Lee handed Mr. Terry his letter from General Jackson.

"Hm. You're Adam Baird's son? How do I know you're entitled to those goods?"

"General Jackson's note says so. And you must have heard of my father being murdered by Deerhide."

"Yes, I did. Sorry about it, too. How many brothers and sisters have you? Where's your mother?"

"My mother is dead, sir. I have no brothers or sisters."

"You mean you're alone in the world? Sure?"

"I'm sure. General Jackson said you would let me have the goods."

"It's irregular, but I suppose I'll have to. Young man," Mr. Terry said, "do you realize what a dangerous trip it is to New Orleans? Do you know that cutthroats and thieves lie in wait along the river for keelboat crews? Do you think you'll ever reach New Orleans, an inexperienced youngster like you?"

"I've heard it isn't easy nor safe, getting there. But I have to. I have to sell my produce."

"Sell it to me. I'll give you eighty dollars right now."

Lee smiled. "No, thank you." The sum offered was only a fraction of what he thought he might get in New Orleans. "May I move the goods as soon as I arrange with Mr. Rawlins?" he added.

Mr. Terry shrugged. "How do you propose paying me for storage?"

"When I return from New Orleans I'll pay you. I have no money now."

Mr. Terry seemed uneasy about his payment. He painted a lurid picture of the dangers of keelboating down-river and of the many temptations awaiting in New Orleans to part a man from his money. He seemed not to have faith that Lee intended returning to Nashville. At last Lee became impatient.

"Sir, do you refuse to release my goods? I have promised to pay when I have funds. I don't care to sell them to you; therefore you will never get paid and can hold them forever if you like. If you are refusing to let me have them, I want to call upon General Jackson again today and ask his help."

The shrewd dark eyes studied him. "Is that what you'd do—run to the General?"

"Yes."

He thought this over. Seizing a pen, he wrote rapidly for a moment, then showed Lee the paper. "Sign this. It promises to pay me one-fifth of the amount you receive on selling your goods in New Orleans. That's more than my storage charges, but I deserve a bit more because I have to wait for my money—if ever I do get it," he added gloomily.

Lee reflected. The storage charge already was almost one-fifth of the minimum amount he thought he might get in New Orleans. Therefore the agreement did not seem unfair.

"I'll sign it, Mr. Terry," he said, "if you will give me the services of a man and a cart tomorrow to move my goods onto a barge."

"Bless me!" The warehouseman stared. Then he seemed to suppress a smile. "If I had folk like you to deal with all day long, I'd soon find myself out of business, I warrant ye!"

Lee signed the paper and gave it back. He took his cap and rose, but Mr. Terry stayed him.

"Young man," he said earnestly, "I want to warn you. I do believe this river trip's become as dangerous as—well, as soldiering against the Indians. As you may learn to the cost of your life, the river is beset with criminals and renegades and murderers. In especial there is the one called Deerhide, who—"

Lee's exclamation stopped him. "But he's around these parts! Is he along the river too?"

"He's been reported between here and Natchez in the last two months, yes. I tell you honestly, lad, I never expect to get paid my storage because I doubt you'll live to sell your goods. 'Tis that bad, without exaggeration."

Lee scarcely heard the last. His eyes held a faraway look and his jaw had firmed at the mention of Deerhide. At length he did meet Mr. Terry's look. "I hope," he said grimly, "that I do meet Deerhide. For I mean to kill him."

Mr. Terry blinked. He seemed about to laugh; then something in his visitor's earnestness prevented him. "Hm. That's large talk for a boy."

"I mean to kill him as he killed my father—and many another."

"Well, if you manage it, I'll not charge a cent for storage."

Lee stepped closer. "Do you mean that? Because for my part, Mr. Terry, I do mean what I say!"

The warehouseman sat blinking up at him. Again he seized paper and pen and scribbled a brief note and signed it. "Here," he said, handing it to Lee. "This says that if you can give me evidence of having rid this country of that foul rascal, Deerhide, I'll not charge you one penny."

Lee folded the note and thrust it inside his shirt. "Mr. Terry," he informed, "you have released me from all storage charge on my goods. I'll prove it on my return. Good day, sir."

He went out. As the fresh air struck his face, he realized that perhaps he had acted the braggart. Certainly he was assuming a great deal, that he, a lad of seventeen, could find and deal with the infamous and wily Deerhide.

Yes, he had out-talked himself. He had virtually promised to accomplish something that no older man, experienced on the river and in the woods, had been able to do. It had been impetuous to talk as he had, and it was his burning hate for Deerhide that had made him.

Lee stared unseeingly down at the water front with its bustle of arriving settlers, stevedores, and barges. If fate would lead him to Deerhide, he would chance the result. He would handle the fellow somehow—else, as Mr. Terry seemed to fear, he would not be alive to return to Nashville!

"Where's old Pickleface?" a voice demanded.

Lee resented the tone even before he saw its roughly dressed and unkempt owner. He was a medium-built individual but somehow stamped with a look of power and daring. A reddish growth on his cheeks thickened at his chin to a scraggly beard. His eyes had a pin-sharp look though they were a little bloodshot as from lack of sleep, and his jaws chomped steadily on a mouthful of tobacco. He spat. "Where's Pickleface, I asked ye!"

The tone and the fellow's uncouthness grated on Lee. "I don't know any Pickleface. And I haven't a mirror to show you," he retorted.

Instantly he regretted his remark. But to his relief, the other did not seem to grasp the insult. "Pickleface, Pickleface!" he snapped. "Terry, of course!"

"Oh." Lee jerked a thumb over his shoulder. "In there. Where's Red Feather Rawlins?" he demanded in the same blunt tone the other had used.

The man started off, glanced back, and turned. "Who wants him? And for what?"

"I want him, else I wouldn't have inquired. I'm going down-river with him."

The fellow's sharp eyes ran over Lee, estimating him. "You're going down-river with 'im? I calc'late not."

"I calculate yes. So does General Jackson."

He chewed his tobacco, gathered a mouthful of juice, and squirted it past Lee's elbow. "Cocky little rooster. Well, goin' down-river'll teach ye different. If ye live. There's men hidin' in wait for the likes of you," he informed. "They'll grind ye up in two bites. Stay home—that's my advice. The advice," he added, "of Red Feather Rawlins."

Lee started. "You—?" His voice broke and he had to try again. "You're—? Phew!"

"Yes, phew, indeed! Now, what makes ye think ye'll go to New Orleans along with me? And why do ye want to?"

"I have cotton and hides and tobacco in this warehouse," Lee returned. "Not a great quantity, but it means much to me to sell them in New Orleans. General Jackson is a friend of mine and he—"

"A friend of yours? How would that be?"

"It happens he is," Lee said firmly. "He suggested that I accompany you, and he said you're leaving day after tomorrow. He said since my produce won't take much space, my work on the boat going down will pay the freight charges. He gave me this," Lee added, bringing the General's note from inside his shirt. "It's for you."

Red Feather Rawlins took it doubtfully. He fingered it and stared at it but seemed uneasy. Suddenly he swore and handed the note back. "Blast ye! I can't read. The General'd ought to know that! What does it say?"

Lee read the brief note introducing him and suggesting that Rawlins include Lee in the crew of his keelboat or see that he got on another in the same flotilla.

When he had finished, Rawlins took the note back and stuffed it in his pocket. "Had any river experience?"

"No," Lee admitted.

Again the other swore. He sighed. "All right,

along ye go. But I guess you'll drown yourself before we're two days out. Can ye handle a gun?"

"As well as anyone."

Annoyance showed in Rawlins's face. "Ye talk too cocky! Ye can't shoot as well as I can—no one can. So don't—"

His attitude so irritated Lee that he spoke as positively as Rawlins. "Of course I can, with a rifle, at least. I can put out a squirrel's eye at fifty yards."

"We'll find out." Rawlins glowered. As if remembering his visit to Mr. Terry, he turned away. "Have your produce on the *Cumberland Belle* before dawn mornin' after next. She's docked yonder." He pointed to a mass of barges and flatboats tied to stumps along the river bank. "We don't wait for anyone, mind. I'll likely be aboard to tell ye where to stow your precious cotton and hides. Come ready for work," he ended sharply, "because work is what ye'll have these next weeks!"

He stalked away. Lee stood watching until he had disappeared within Mr. Terry's warehouse. Then turning, he walked thoughtfully to where he had tied Venus.

On his way back to the livery barn he kept puzzling over Red Feather Rawlins. That name—why was he called Red Feather? His beard, of course, was reddish. But Lee had not observed any feather on him—say by way of decoration. Well, what's in a name?

The man was insolent in his manner and snarling tone. He had a foul mouth, larding everything he said with fierce oaths. Yet there was something Lee had to admire about him—his vigor, perhaps. He looked and acted like one who would plunge into work or danger without pausing to think of fatigue or fear. He was a devil-may-care fellow; he seemed to have the attitude that he was as good as any man who walked—and better than most.

Under his boldness and bluster, Lee thought, there was something hidden. Something that Red Feather Rawlins was being bold so as to conceal. It was just an idea, and doubtless wrong. But that was how Rawlins impressed Lee.

He quit the livery with some regret, for Mr. Roston had given him a job when he needed it badly. He was even a little sorry to leave Emil, the fat and usually surly foreman, for Lee had learned how to get along with him. Mr. Roston wished him well as he paid Lee off. Emil only glowered and did not offer to shake hands.

All that Wednesday Lee labored to get his produce aboard the *Cumberland Belle*. She was a huge, ungainly craft built of hand-adzed planks cut upstream a way. Some forty feet long and eighteen wide, she was a floating platform for goods with a lean-to shelter of light poles near her stern. There, on a flooring of crude bricks a fire could be built for cooking. Her deck gradually filled with bales of cotton and bundles of tobacco leaves brought by solid-wheel drays from The Hermitage—for the *Belle* would carry only General Jackson's goods save for the small quantity of Lee's.

"Is this what's called a keelboat?" Lee asked Rawlins.

"She is."

"Why's she called a keelboat?"

"Because, thickhead, she has a keel. Makes her easier to manage. A craft this size has got to be manageable, doesn't she?"

"Well, do you mean those smaller ones haven't keels?" He indicated the log-built craft clustered around them.

"Few have. A keel's good on any boat. But it's scarce worth buildin' on small ones, seeing as they get throwed away anyhow."

"Thrown away? You mean they aren't brought back from New Orleans?"

Rawlins gestured as if pleading with heaven for patience. "You just don't know *any*thing! Of course they don't bring 'em back, And this craft won't be brought back. How'd you like to pole a flatboat two thousand miles against the current? It'd take years! So they break up the craft in New Orleans, and we walk back or ride horses along the Natchez Trace, which is a road. But I suppose you'll fly," he sneered. "You'll want something different."

Lee shook his head. It did seem wasteful to build

a new flatboat every time produce was to be taken down-river to New Orleans. Still, there was, as Rawlins said, only poling to move a craft upstream. Towing from shore doubtless would not work for overhanging trees and irregularities of the bank. So all these craft in tomorrow's flotilla would be broken up for timber when the trip was over. That was how it worked.

General Jackson's Negro hostler came for Venus late that afternoon. He waited while Lee stood petting her and swallowing hard and blinking to keep back threatening tears. As if she sensed something out of the ordinary was about to happen, Venus nuzzled him and gently butted his chest and let him stroke under her arching neck.

Suddenly, Lee threw his arms around her and kissed her. Then, his eyes blurring, he led her out of the fenced yard, gave her halter rope to the Negro and ran into the barn so he would not have to watch her being taken away. But he could not resist a look out as she went trotting briskly off behind the hostler's horse.

Lee watched, his throat crowded with a heavy lump, until she was out of sight. He wondered if he would ever see Venus again.

CHAPTER SEVEN

NEW ORLEANS BOUND

The orange streaks of dawn were lengthening into the overhead sky when, having spent his last night in the livery barn mow, Lee walked rapidly down the hill from Nashville to Johnson's Landing. It was chill and damp this morning in early October, with lazy masses of mist completely hiding the Cumberland River and the barges along its banks.

As he followed the winding dusty road he heard and could vaguely see other persons hurrying toward the river, many of them bent under heavy packs. A team of mules pulling a two-wheeled cart loaded with cotton passed him and he quickened his step, apprehensive lest the flotilla depart without him.

Following Mr. Roston's advice, Lee had spent the few dollars he possessed on equipment. The river trip commonly required thirty to forty-five days and there was no place this side of Natchez to buy anything. The second-hand heavy coat he wore already was proving welcome, and he knew it would be needed during rain and on cold nights.

Wrapped in the bulky blanket he carried on one shoulder were a few cooking and eating utensils and some food. While small game might be encountered en route, and various wild fowls usually were available, men who made the trip reported that at times no game was to be found. So Lee had a supply of jerked meat, a loaf of bread, some hardtack, a sack of dried vegetables, and a pouch of ground acorns for brewing the coffee substitute.

General Jackson's hostler had brought him a rifle and a supply of powder and shot. Lee felt relieved and grateful for the gift, for both Mr. Roston and Emil had called it the height of folly to undertake such a trip without a weapon. It was a long, heavy rifle, by no means new nor even of late design, but Lee felt sure it would shoot straight enough. He certainly had need of it—and it was a handsome gift for General Jackson to make.

Part-way down the hill he stopped. The blanket holding his belongings made an awkward bundle and he had some difficulty shifting it to his other shoulder. Stooping, he picked up his rifle, then resumed walking, holding it out and looking at it.

"I'm going to name you General," he said. "I certainly was worried about not having a gun, but Jehoshaphat, I just didn't have money for one!"

Aided by a light breeze, the mists around the river were dissolving. As he plodded down to the landing, sounds of wagon wheels, shouted orders, and the thump of freight became louder. When the sun abruptly came out brightly, Lee found a scene of seeming confusion some three hundred yards along the river.

His eyes widened. "It must be a regular fleet that's going!"

And it did look that way, judging by the dozen craft on which men busily stowed away goods as if preparing to depart. There were small barges that two men could handle, larger ones already so covered with bales and barrels that little deck space remained, and finally the big *Cumberland Belle* which held General Jackson's goods. Lee could see his own five bales of cotton and his carefully boxed leaf tobacco and a thick wired pad of hides there near the stern on the *Belle's* river side.

He picked his way among carts, stands of freight and groups of men and women until he reached the rough timbers that made a gangplank to the *Belle*. Lee stood there a moment, taking in the scene.

Tall, bronzed frontier farmers were bidding their wives good-by and giving last-minute instructions. A stevedore boss shouted at three Negroes and a team of mules that had come near dumping several bales of cotton into the river. Knots of men stood smoking and talking; aboard the barges other men were re-stowing cargo, calling to each other cheerfully or angrily as they made ready.

He found Red Feather Rawlins directing three men on the *Belle* as they rearranged some of the cargo. Rawlins wore his same ill-kempt costume of yesterday, but in surprise Lee saw that his battered fur cap was missing. Today Rawlins wore his long, greasy, black hair Indian style, with a two-inch ribbon of vari-colored beads around his forehead. In it, over one ear, rode a vivid red feather.

That explained his nickname—this affectation Rawlins had. No doubt he considered himself dressed for river life when he had on that feather. It seemed to indicate that despite his unwashed appearance, he had a certain peculiar vanity.

"What the devil ye standin' there for?" he roared.

Lee realized Rawlins was addressing him. Quickly he picked his way to the gangplank and mounted it to the barge. Red Feather Rawlins waited, hands on hips, a sneer turning back his wide lips.

"I hope we didn't get ye out o' bed too early? Or cause ye any inconveniencc?"

Two of the three men on the keelboat with him grinned widely. Rawlins gestured at Lee as he turned to them. "Looks like we got a gentleman aboard. Well—" He surveyed Lee with a leer. "Ye won't look nor feel like a gentleman by nightfall. This here is hard, wearin' work!

"Throw your blanket down!" he roared as Lee made no reply. "Get over and clear those barrels from the steerin' oar! How in seven devils d'ye think we can control the craft while it's choked up with goods? If ye aim to ride the *Belle,*" he warned over waving forefinger, "pitch in and do your share. Or

"Throw Your Blanket Down," He Roared

I'll heave ye in the river!"

Anger blazed inside Lee but he decided it was best to make no retort. He passed Red Feather Rawlins half expecting the fellow would reach out and cuff him, or at least trip him. But nothing happened, and Lee went to the lean-to where he saw other blankets piled, and put his own down.

"Want to help me move those barrels?"

Lee found a man of perhaps twenty-one or twenty-two looking him over. He was well over six feet tall and was extraordinarily gangly, but he looked fit and hard. And he had twinkling blue eyes and limp, flaxen hair, and a note of cheeriness about him.

"Glad to. Where do they get moved to?" Lee stepped to the other's side and went with him to a cluster of barrels, the pungent odors they emitted suggesting they contained herbs, perhaps for medicines.

"I'm Homer Hannibal Smith. That's it—guess you know how to roll barrels, eh? What's your name?" he asked as they fell to work.

"Lee Baird." Their eyes met and Lee grinned. "You've really got a great name," he said.

"Terrible name. My father was a scholar." He jerked his head. "The red feather fellow—is he as tough as his roars'd make me think?"

"I'm not sure. I sort of think he is." He added as they turned back for more barrels: "Have you ever been down-river?"

"Once. Anyhow, down almost to Natchez. Then some river-beaters robbed us of everything. Except my rifle and the clothes I stood in," he corrected. "I walked most of the way home—along the Natchez Trace. A year's labor gone."

Lee stared. "How'd that happen?"

They were again rolling barrels side by side.

Homer Hannibal Smith shrugged. "It can happen, all right. Those fellows'll kill without saying howdy-do. There are gangs of them. We put ashore when we saw a man standing on the bank naked as the day he was born, and shouting for help. It was a decoy, of course. But how could we tell?" He shrugged. "We didn't like to pass a man if he really was in trouble."

They worked a few minutes in silence. Apprehension clouded Lee's face, for Homer's experience had an ominous sound. "You say it cost a year's work?"

"A whole year's produce. Hides and cotton. So I lost my farm. Couldn't pay for it, you see. I got back in fall, trapped all winter, and took another farm in spring. That was a year ago. And here I am."

Lee thought this over. "Well, I hope we don't get robbed!"

Homer mopped his forehead with his ragged homespun sleeve. "Big keelboat like this, heavily loaded, makes a wonderful prize. Those river-beaters are slick sometimes, the way they lure you ashore. Other times when you tie up for firewood or to shoot some game, they ambush you and kill you off—" he snapped his fingers "—like that. And if you do get to New Orleans safely and sell your goods—"

Lee swallowed. "Then what?"

"I've heard New Orleans is the hardest city in the world to keep money in. Footpads. All kinds of skin games. Fancy ladies being sweet to you till they poison you or knock you out, then take your money. Even if you get out of New Orleans with it, you've still got to get home."

"Is that hard?"

"Men getting killed all the time. Ambushes along the road. Strangers joining you at supper to find out how well armed you are and how much money you have. They're in league with toughs hiding and watching you.

"Yes," Homer declared, "it's all a hard working man can do to raise a little cotton. But that's only half. Selling it in New Orleans and then getting home with the money is the other half."

They heard a shout and saw that the foremost barge down-river had cast off. Red Feather Rawlins was bawling to the two other men who seemed to make up the *Belle's* crew, and they ran to the twisted vines that served as ropes holding the keelboat to the shore. As Rawlins bellowed an order and gestured, Lee and Homer ran to the stern vines.

Rawlins, watching his crew, picked his way among bales and barrels to the great steering oar in the stern. "Come over here, you!" he yelled to Lee.

He obeyed quickly. "You ever handle a steerin' oar? No—no! Stand on the other side of 't," he snarled as Lee came beside him. "I guess you won't be much good—you gentleman," he sneered.

He watched two barges ahead of them slowly washed into the muddy stream. "All right—let go!" Rawlins ordered Homer and the two older men. As they did so, Rawlins maneuvered the forty-foot steering oar which lay in a stout-built oarlock of hickory over the stern. "Lean to it!" he snapped.

Lee did, striving to guess how Rawlins would move next. They strained and shoved and managed to move slowly the long, narrow hemlock trunk onto whose water end short boards had been bolted to make a sweep. The handle end had been skinned of bark but was too thick for a good hand-hold, so that pushing or pulling from side to side was the only means of control. Apparently slowly swishing it was what Rawlins wanted. Lee saw that the narrow expanse of river between the keelboat and the bank was gradually widening.

The sluggish current seemed to grasp the keelboat in strong hands. She swung a little sideways as if the river was going to twist her completely around.

"Hey!" bawled Rawlins. He put his chest against

the oar, and Lee pulled on it with all his might. A tall, gray-grizzled man came running and added his strength. With muscle-straining work they managed to correct the barge's twist and get her headed parallel with the shore.

"Hold her there. She's got a keel—she'll steer if there's always somebody got his eyes open. Here, Kelso," Rawlins growled to a short, thick, muscular man whose left eyelid sagged in a way that gave his pinched features a wry expression, as if he had unexpectedly swallowed a mouthful of pickles. "Grab on here!"

Kelso replaced him at the steering oar. He gave orders in a quiet voice. The tall, gray man said no word but he also seemed experienced in managing the oar.

"Phew!" Lee exclaimed, dripping with sweat.

Kelso flicked one eyebrow. "Green, eh? This here's a big craft, biggest I ever went on, almost. Your arms'll feel like they're dropping off tomorrow. Shoulders too. Eh, John Beaver?"

"Eh," was all Beaver said. Nor during the whole voyage did Lee hear him speak more than two sentences at one time.

"I wish I could catch on to this. I don't understand it!" Lee confessed.

"Day or two 'n' you'll get the feel o' the river. It'll come sudden, like ridin' a hoss." Kelso jerked his head to where Red Feather Rawlins and Homer

Smith were shifting cargo so the keelboat would ride evenly. "He growls like a hungry grizzly. But you jump when he orders, and I reckon he won't chaw you."

Lee was glad to know this, for he had not sized up Rawlins satisfactorily. He was not drawn to his personality, that was sure. Still, he would have to get along with the man.

"He's in charge," Lee reflected.

Kelso nodded. "Leads the whole flotilla."

"If they stay together, like they agreed," John Beaver said.

Now, for the first time with the two experienced men working the sweep with him, Lee had opportunity to gaze around. All the barges on which there had been bustle at Johnson's Landing had not cast off with them. One had cast off first, a fair-sized craft now almost a mile ahead. Three more were trailing the *Belle,* which was much the largest of the five.

"Have we got more crew than the others?" Lee asked.

Kelso glanced up-river, then down-river. He spat tobacco juice into the oarlock, for friction of the sweep occasionally brought a wisp of smoke curling from it.

"We got five. Couple of 'em got three or four. One's only got two men."

"This is the only one with a keel?"

"Nope. One followin's got a keel."

"Can we cook aboard here? Or do we always have to tie up?"

"Cook long's we got grub. Ain't so bad to tie up 'tween here and the Ohio," Kelso said. "Gets more risky after that. Bushwhackers 'n' river-beaters. Can't tell where. Purty safe down to about where we'll run outa grub," he explained. "When you need game, it's takin' risks to go ashore'n get it. You cook?" he added.

"Yes, pretty well."

"Hey, Rawlins!" When the chief of their party looked around, Kelso pointed to Lee. "Cooks, he says."

"He's our cook, then," Rawlins decided. "Don't mean he gets out o' no work, though. Go'n' get a fire started," he told Lee shortly.

Leaving the sweep with some relief, Lee moved puzzledly toward the lean-to, a simple shelter made of trimmed branches. He found boxes and casks clustered there containing salt, flour, bacon, dried beef, crackers, potatoes, beans and other hardy food items. Fresh water was available in four hogsheads near-by. There were half a dozen sacks of charcoal from which, he judged, he was to maintain the fire when lengths of wood were not available. There was a crude brick platform some four by four feet on which the fire would lie, the entire keelboat being of wood.

He set about building a fire and soon was thrusting in six-inch logs to hold it. Lee set up two folding iron-bar tripods, one on either side of the fire, and placed a bar between them. Meat could be roasted over this or kettles hung on it.

The lean-to, he saw now, was intended to shelter only their food. It was not large enough to also house any of the crew, who evidently lived entirely out of doors. The few personal belongings of the five men lay huddled against the lean-to.

Homer Smith loitered with Lee later on. "Have some grub about an hour before overhead sun," he suggested. "Can you make a stew? There's always stew ready on a keelboat. Rawlins'll divide us in shifts, see, so there's always two men at the sweep, night and day, 'less we're tied up."

Lee could make a stew of potatoes, vegetables, and beef, and set about doing it. Red Feather Rawlins came and watched him a moment but made no comment. In a way, his silence was a definite compliment for Lee knew he would have criticized fast enough if he thought he saw anything wrong.

Rawlins wandered about the slow-moving keelboat to make sure everything was in order. Kelso and John Beaver were still at the sweep. Homer Smith sat on a barrel up front, vigilant for sand bars and now and then calling back directions for making sharp turns in the river.

It was a sunny, almost cloudless day. If the

weather held like this, the trip should not be a bad one, Lee thought. That is, if there was no encounter with the scoundrels waiting to prey on honest men and rob them of the fruits of months of labor.

Rawlins stomped up behind him. He tasted the stew, tipped the bucket, and poured a generous helping into his wooden plate. He sat down and ate ravenously without speaking. When he finished the acorn brew he looked almost cheerful.

"How do ye like keelboatin', son?"

"Reckon I'll like it fine. 'Course, I know I'm not handy on a boat yet. But I'll try to learn."

"Stupid men can learn. Mebbe you can too." Rising, Rawlins pushed Lee's shoulder and grinned a little. Then he went to a spot where the lean-to would shade him, spread a dirty blanket on the deck, and lay down on it. It seemed only a minute before his long, slow snores proved him asleep.

Time passed. It was a lazy, bright October day. Lee was drowsy and could have slept but felt he should soon relieve one of the men at the steering oar. He had fed them and Homer.

Red Feather Rawlins moved restlessly. Something was making him uncomfortable, though not enough so to bring him fully awake. He fumbled inside his shirt and moved something there. A few moments later he fumbled again, and brought out two stunted, stubby pistols and laid them beside him. They were not as large as a man's hand and might be toys, Lee thought, save that they had such an ugly look.

But why two of them? And Rawlins had a fine rifle, he knew, and a regular-size pistol, too. And the knife he carried in his boot had looked razor sharp when Lee had glimpsed it that morning.

He stared at the small pistols, then at the sleeping man's face. There was something strange and—yes, disquieting about Red Feather Rawlins. He seemed an odd choice for General Andrew Jackson to make for his agent. However, he must be trustworthy or the General would not have put him in charge of this big keelboat and all the produce from The Hermitage to be marketed in New Orleans.

Lee's heart stopped, then resumed its beat hurriedly. Red Feather Rawlins was awake and regarding him. He knew he had spied the pistols. His eyes were slitted and glinting and Lee did not like their inscrutable look.

Wrenching his gaze away, Lee turned to stir his stew, trying to pretend he had not noticed Rawlins awake and was not aware of the fellow slyly thrusting those two gambler's pistols back inside his shirt.

A chill quivered down Lee's back. He could not explain it. He just disliked that man—yes, and feared him, too.

CHAPTER EIGHT

DEERHIDE AGAIN

It was as hard labor managing the keelboat, Lee found, as working on his father's farm had been—and the labor here went on nights as well as days. He had supposed there would be little to do save let the current push the ungainly craft downstream, perhaps guiding her so as always to keep in deep water. But there was a great deal more to keelboating than that.

The Cumberland was a river of myriad twists and turns. It was deep enough when it abruptly changed direction, but often these elbows were uncomfortably narrow. The smaller barges of the flotilla maneuvered with comparative ease where the *Belle* had tree branches brushing her sides. Sometimes, to keep her from nosing into the soft banks men had to leap ashore and tug with all their might to control her with bow or stern ropes in coordination with the pair working furiously at the big steering oar.

Where the river was widest it was likely to have unexpected shallows. There always had to be a lookout forward watching for sand bars and shoals. Several times during the first week the *Belle* almost pushed herself fast on a bar. Then Red Feather Rawlins bellowed orders and Lee, Homer, Kelso, and the silent John Beaver poled frantically along her sides to fend her off.

Once, just before sunset, Rawlins was asleep when this happened. There was a good expanse of water on either side, but suddenly there was a faint rustling sound and the heavily loaded craft came to a grudging halt.

Awakened instantly, Rawlins scrambled to his feet. He gave a wide, encompassing glance that told him the danger just as the cry, "Sand bar!" came from up front.

"Pole her back—quick!" Rawlins yelled at Beaver and Homer at the sweep. "Lee, you lazy rascal, tumble out! Kelso, pole on her quarter. No—to the right! Pole her off!"

Seizing a rope fastened at the stern, he ran to the edge and leaped onto a narrow sandy island. Digging his heels into the ground and leaning far back, he tugged with all his might. Meanwhile a shout came from the smaller barge following, and Lee's glance back showed it bearing down on them.

"*Pole!*" Rawlins roared, red-faced with his effort.

If the following barge struck, she would force the *Belle* farther up on the bar. She swept within twenty yards . . . fifteen . . . Her crew worked frantically to alter her course and the five-man crew of the *Belle* labored as frantically on their own craft.

The following barge cleared the *Belle's* stern quarter by a man's length. She passed on downriver. Meanwhile the *Belle* reluctantly slid into deeper water. She seemed suddenly to take her head, as Lee had known Venus to do when she wanted to run, and sailed along with the current so rapidly that Rawlins was stranded. His mouth got full exercise as he waded from sandspit to sandspit, finally got ashore, and ran along it after the barge. He kept vanishing behind trees and shrubs, reappearing, watching for a narrows where he could leap back aboard.

When he did rejoin them, soaked and muddy, he was in an ugly mood. Lee could not be sure what or who Rawlins was cursing—the river, the barge that had almost struck them, or his own men. At any rate it was best to keep out of his way, say nothing, and pay strict attention to duty. After a while Rawlins went back to the lean-to and stretched out for another hour's sleep.

The trouble was, Lee told Homer that evening, the smaller barges ought to be ahead of the *Belle*. "Sooner or later we might get badly grounded. We draw more water than they do. Then they might slam right into us."

"I mentioned that the day we left," Homer said, twisting himself a crude cigar of tobacco leaves. "Rawlins told me to shut my mouth. Maybe now he sees it for himself."

Rawlins did see it, but the next day when the *Belle* tied up and the smaller barges swept past despite his snarled orders for them also to stop, he seemed greatly upset.

"I meant 'em to still keep with us!" he raged, walking up and down and viciously snapping a small branch over his thigh. "Look—they'll be clear out o' sight tomorrow! The fools! We started as a group; we ought to stay that way. Lot safer against bushwhackers, ain't it?"

Lee knew he was correct in this. Yet Rawlins ranted on so long about the *Belle* being left behind that even John Beaver decided the matter called for a few words. "They're gone. We can't do anything."

"Yeah," Rawlins snapped, "they're gone, and it'll serve 'em right if they're gutted. Then they'll whine for help—want clothes and grub and maybe even money. Wait'll everything they got belongs to river pirates and they're stark naked and starvin'—if they ain't corpses!"

As if to bear out Rawlins's fears, two days later one of the barges was found grounded and burned to the water's edge. When the *Belle* nosed ashore and her whole crew went to examine the wreck they found one body, naked. There was nothing else—no sign of her other two crewmen nor of the goods the barge had held.

Rawlins spat. "There. What'd I tell ye?"

"I wonder if it was Deerhide's gang?"

Rawlins looked sharply at Lee. "Deerhide? He ain't along the river, he's back around Nashville."

"I heard he was along the river."

"Wal, he ain't. Lot more things blamed on Deerhide'n he ever done. Let's get started again. Come on!"

The five men had worked out a schedule which kept two at the steering oar and one as lookout at all times the craft was in the current. That left two men always resting. On the few occasions the *Belle* tied up to trees on the bank for the night, four were off duty, the fifth sitting with his rifle over his knees as watchman.

Lee, while doing his full part in shifting cargo when necessary, standing watch, and manning the steering oar, also had the cooking to do. He got no relief from other chores for this—nor, he reflected with irritation, any thanks. Hot water for acorn brew and some hot dish were expected to be ready at all times. What the hot dish was did not matter —a stew, a thick soup, potatoes and jerked meat, or whatnot.

"Stew's gone," Kelso reminded Lee, wiping traces of it from his heavy black bristles.

Their meat almost gone, Lee suggested to Rawlins that they had better save some in case of need.

"What do you want?"

"I could go ashore and maybe get some ducks.

Red Feather Looked Sharply at Lee

We've seen lots of them heading south. Or a few squirrels, or maybe pheasants."

"All right," Rawlins shrugged, and started to turn away.

"Just a minute. It's my time off now and I'm sleepy," Lee said. "Do I get to sleep later if I go hunting?"

Rawlins's eyes narrowed in the way that always made a chill slide down Lee's spine. "We got to work this boat. You can't sneak out o' your share o' work because you go hunting."

"I've been doing my share and the cooking too. If you want food ready every time somebody—"

He broke off as Rawlins stepped nearer. Impulsively Lee retreated; then, ashamed of that, he held his ground. Rawlins's face was redder than usual and he stood with his chest almost touching Lee's.

"Listen, you're no good on this boat, not a bit o' good. You don't know a steerin' oar from a sand bar! We'd be just as well off if I'd pitch ye overside. Yes, and maybe—"

Kelso strolled near then with Homer Smith close behind him.

Something in their manner made Red Feather Rawlins eye them sharply and hesitate.

"Goin' huntin', Lee?" Homer asked.

"Fresh meat'd taste pretty good. Eh, Rawlins? 'Course," Kelso said, "if it takes you long to get somethin', we'll split up your work so's you get a chance to sleep."

Rawlins seemed debating whether to snarl curses at them or drop the matter. Lee did not like the look of him, the way his face was changing from deep red to blackish. He was relieved when General Jackson's agent ended the scene with a curt laugh as he turned away. "I'll be surprised if Lee can hit anything smaller'n the *Belle,*" he sneered.

Kelso returned to the steering oar, but Homer lingered while Lee got his rifle and loaded it. Homer talked casually about his hope that Lee would find some ducks. They walked to the edge of the barge and Lee watched his chance to leap ashore.

Their eyes met. "I don't like him," Lee growled.

"No? Why?"

"I don't quite know. But he's a bully. If you hadn't come along I think he'd have wanted to fight. And of course he thought he could wipe up the boat with me—then toss me in the river."

"The kind of fighting these rivermen do is pretty bad," Homer reminded. "They'll cut you to ribbons or spill you and then bring both heels down in your face. How do you think you'd come out?"

Lee shrugged. "Anyhow, I don't like him. It isn't the work," he explained. "It's as if he carries a grudge, and I don't know why. Do you feel that?"

Homer glanced around to make sure they were not overheard. "You really don't know why Rawlins watches you like a cat does a mouse? He's General Jackson's agent, ain't he?"

"Yes. But what—?"

"He thinks you're secretly the General's agent too—sent to watch Red Feather Rawlins."

Lee cocked his head. "He does? But—what makes him think that? I'm not—not at all!"

Homer indicated a jut of bank coming nearer, and Lee got ready to jump ashore. "From different things Rawlins has dropped, I take it he suspects you're here to spy on him. Better not refer to it—he won't believe whatever you say. Jump!" Homer urged.

It was difficult to bring down many ducks with a rifle, since each report sent the flight wheeling aloft. The *Belle* swam slowly out of sight while Lee patiently awaited his chance; then he was lucky enough to get two with the same ball. But it took him nearly an hour to retrieve them in soggy marshland. Plastered with mud, he hurried after the keelboat, easily killing five squirrels, one by one, as he went. It was dark when he caught up with the boat, which for a time had been mired in a soft bank.

Everyone aboard it was short-tempered, but sight of Lee's game improved matters. He roasted the ducks and one squirrel, and when the men had eaten they were all in better humor.

The Mississippi was a wide, shallow expanse of sluggish water.

It was monotonous to look at. Life aboard the

keelboat was uncomfortable and the labor often exhausting. When the *Belle* wedged firmly on a sand bar in midstream and clung there a whole day despite the perspiring work of her crew, tempers frayed almost to the breaking point. Indeed, Kelso and Homer were squaring away for a fight that might have had an ugly outcome when constant prodding with the poles suddenly crumbled the sand and released the *Belle*.

A long month had passed since leaving Nashville, and the fact was that monotony was wearing the nerves of all. They were tired of the uneven diet as game first proved plentiful, and then became so scarce as to put them on short rations. The men were restless at confinement to the keelboat, and weary of constantly seeing each other.

All of them were, that is, except Red Feather Rawlins. He seemed to Lee to have an undercurrent of cheerfulness, though on the surface he acted as dissatisfied as ever with his crew. Lee had almost forgotten the uneasiness he had felt about the two concealed pistols Rawlins carried when they tied up on the thirty-second night.

"Might be in for a blow," Rawlins had said late that afternoon, scanning the sky. "Reckon we'll tie up yonder." He pointed to a wide pool of quiet water where the mighty river made a turn.

It surprised Lee. He almost countered that he did not expect much wind, and that nothing short of a gale had heretofore been cause to tie up. But he kept silent, glad enough for a quiet night.

They scattered ashore until darkness brought them back. Silent John Beaver fished from a steep bank and brought in eight good-sized bullheads and two carp. Homer shot a small wild pig, and Kelso half a dozen squirrels. Rawlins said he had not seen any game. Lee, guarding the keelboat from the bank, had shot three pheasant.

After a hearty supper the men turned in, except Rawlins, whose turn it was to stand watch. Lee, though, had got a nap that afternoon, and after an hour of vainly trying to sleep tossed his blanket aside and rose.

He gazed around at the dark river. The thin eighth of moon was hazy and its curve would hold water, he saw. That meant rain coming. He moved to lean on the steering oar and fell to wondering what New Orleans would be like, and when they would be there.

So far they had seen no sign of bushwhackers and he wondered if tales of their depredations were not greatly exaggerated. Certainly he hoped so, for his goods aboard the *Cumberland Belle* were his total wealth. He depended heavily on the money he hoped to get for them to provide for his future.

He wondered how General Jackson was faring, whether he had regained his health and strength. Doubtless he was on his way south to Fort Mims in Mississippi Territory now. Lee did not think he could quite have reached it, although by coasting down various rivers and by forced marches—

A flash of light attracted him. It seemed to come from the spot ashore where Red Feather Rawlins had been seated on a fallen tree on guard.

Lee waited. He saw it again—briefly, a yellowish light that blinked and was gone.

Frowning, he moved across the keelboat. From a new position he could vaguely see a dark form. That would be Rawlins. He was standing on the fallen tree and seemed to have his arms raised around his chest.

Lee wondered if he had imagined those two blinks of light. "Pshaw, guess I must have!"

But he could not convince himself of this. On impulse he moved along the side of the keelboat until he could jump nimbly and silently ashore. Then he moved farther along the bank and crouched low and waited.

Now he could make out Rawlins's muscular form against the slightly paler sky. Again a yellow light came from something he held. It blinked rather long, then gave shorter blinks. It was, Lee guessed, a black-lamp, consisting of a three-inch thick candle with a tin door that could be opened and closed quickly. Several of the lamps were aboard the keelboat for use at night in picking one's way among bales and barrels of the cargo; and especially, the watchman always had one for making his occasional rounds.

Lee suppressed an ejaculation. For in the distance, from a hilltop, he judged, came a faint answering light. It was on a matter of seconds, then blinked out. But there it came again! A series of blinks like pin-point yellow dots.

Rawlins answered with a long signal. Then there was darkness.

As minutes passed Lee wondered whether he was dreaming. He pinched himself—but yes, he certainly was awake. He touched the earth where he stood as additional proof that he actually was here, some forty feet from Red Feather Rawlins.

Excitement started in his stomach. It was a prickling sensation that spread until it was skipping down his arms and legs. If those lights blinking back and forth were what he thought—and they *must* be!

He stood intently watching the spot where he knew Rawlins was, though he could not see him now. At last Lee nodded to himself, turned, and stole softly aboard the keelboat. He felt his way among boxes and bales until he gained the stern where the other three crewmen slept soundly near the lean-to. Lee knelt close beside Homer and was about to shake him gently when he heard a low foot-fall.

In panic he snatched his blanket, stretched out, and pretended to be fast asleep like the others.

Through slitted eyes he watched Rawlins's dark form loom near. The man stood looking down at them. Finally, silent as a wraith, Rawlins moved away.

Lee waited. He heard a light thud as Rawlins jumped onto the bank. Getting up then, Lee knelt beside Homer and shook him.

"Homer, wake up!" he whispered.

Homer responded so abruptly that his head struck Lee's shoulder. "Ssh! Listen! I'm not certain, but I think we're going to be attacked!"

"Eh?"

Kelso stirred. "We going to cast off?" He sat up. "What you fellows doing?"

Lee knew that John Beaver also was awake: he could sense the gaunt older man listening. Quickly Lee reported the signals he had seen from the hill-top. He told how they had been answered by Red Feather Rawlins.

There was silence.

"You've had a nightmare." Kelso moved as if to lie down again. "Go to sleep, lad."

"But it wasn't! I pinched myself and even felt of the ground. I tell you, he answered their signals—in fact, he gave the first ones!"

A pause. "Red Feather Rawlins did?"

"Is he doing it now?" Homer demanded.

"No. He's just come past here to make sure we're all asleep. I tell you," Lee urged excitedly, "something's up! We'd better—"

"He's General Jackson's agent," John Beaver reminded.

"Sure he is. He wouldn't be a bushwhacker then!" Kelso derided.

"General Jackson is not a fool," Beaver said.

"I don't know whether the General's deceived in him or not. I'm not trying to explain it," Lee told them impatiently. "But why would Rawlins signal? Who'd be in this lonely country to answer? It's mighty strange, isn't it? And dangerous?"

Homer got to his feet. "Even if Lee's out of his senses, we can only lose some sleep," he told the others. "Of course you're wrong somehow, Lee, because Rawlins must be dependable or the General would not have put him in charge of almost a fortune in goods."

"Stay awake anyhow," Lee urged. "I'm going back and scout a little."

He left them, rifle in hand now, padded along the river side of the keelboat to its bow, then across its width to stand a moment listening and staring into the dark. Presumably Rawlins was back at his post although Lee could not locate him. After some thought, he climbed to the bank. With great caution he went toward the fallen tree on which Rawlins had sat.

Lee touched it with his hand. He still could not see General Jackson's agent. Evidently Rawlins had not returned here. Then was he still aboard the *Belle* and likely to discover Lee's absence? Or was he somewhere—

Lee's pulse halted, then pounded hard.

Voices. They were only a matter of yards away. And they were unfamiliar voices—save one.

Lee padded with Indian stealth the length of the tree. Standing abreast its great clump of roots, he clearly heard men conferring in low tones. He could not catch their words but mentally counted the different voices. Four, five, six—yes, six, he felt sure.

He felt cold all over as he stood gripping his rifle at the ready. He thought of firing it as a warning to his crew comrades. Better, though, to steal back to them so they could surprise the boarders when they came.

The feel of someone dangerously near came over Lee. He stood statue-like.

"—yell out or shoot, Deerhide. We'll come tumblin' aboard!"

"All right. Knives are the tool, boys. Use 'em deep and hard. Remember, dead men can't talk!"

Lee's brain felt watery. He stood for an instant frozen by that terrible revelation.

Deerhide! That fellow had called Rawlins *Deerhide!*

Red Feather Rawlins, trusted agent of General Jackson, was the infamous scoundrel who had murdered Lee's father!

CHAPTER NINE

RIVER BATTLE

The thing was incredible. Yet it must be true!

Lee stood indecisive a moment. Impulse urged him to advance toward the spot from which he had heard Rawlins's voice and to settle with him at once. But reason warned that Rawlins must have moved. Lee might not be able to locate him readily. Hearing him advance, Rawlins would have an advantage.

Besides, he had to consider the safety of his comrades. They were not expecting the notorious Deerhide. They were in danger of being murdered.

And there was the big keelboat loaded with goods. Some was Lee's, and he could not afford its loss. The bulk of the cargo was General Jackson's and, with Rawlins proved traitorous, Lee had a feeling the General's property devolved into his care. He must keep it safe from Red Feather Rawlins, alias Deerhide.

All this sped through his mind in a few seconds. Turning, he crept stealthily back aboard the *Cumberland Belle,* his heavy rifle gripped and ready in case he bumped into one of Deerhide's men. He made it aboard without a sound, halted to listen, then started aft to warn Homer and the others. He had taken but a few steps when—

"Lee?"

He almost brained the dark figure suddenly close in front of him, but in the nick of time he recognized that voice.

"Homer? Listen. Rawlins is Deerhide! They're going to attack us any second. Get up front and pick 'em off when they come. Quick!"

Homer hesitated. Lee could feel his incredulity like an electric force. But Homer was quick-thinking and he must have realized that Lee had reason for his astounding assertion. "All right!" He was gone without a sound.

Lee wondered if Kelso and John Beaver had gone back to sleep near the lean-to. He decided to go and warn them, but after two steps collided with someone.

"Who is it?" he demanded.

No reply came. Instinct made Lee hurriedly fall back and sideways. He was just in time, for a blade whipped through the air, its point catching the sleeve of his homespun shirt and slitting it several inches.

Lee tried to bring his gun up but its long barrel struck his foe. He used the weapon as a prod, jabbing and swishing it left and right in savage blows.

"Bushwhackers!" he shouted. "*It's Deerhide!* Help!"

Next instant he lost his grip on the rifle. His antagonist stabbed again with his knife, and it seemed to hiss close past his cheek. With not time to draw his own from his boot, Lee charged. As they slammed together he heard a shot, then a roared-out warning from Homer:

"They're comin' aboard! Rawlins is Deerhide!"

Two more shots crackled with accompanying red flashes of powder. Scrambling sounds; curses and thuds of colliding bodies; a gasp of pain . . .

Lee scarcely heard. He was locked in fierce tussle with a short, powerful individual. The fellow was striving to drive his knife into Lee's chest. With one hand on the bushwhacker's throat, the other imprisoning his wrist, Lee was compelled to give ground until he felt a bale of cotton at his back. The other was stronger than he and slowly, despite his straining fingers, was wrenching his knife-hand around into position. Lee felt its sharp tip lightly against his chest.

With a desperate last twist of the thick wrist he crouched and gave a violent jerk aside. It broke his hold on the wrist, but also stopped the fellow's short, hard blows to Lee's face. Lee darted away, had time to turn, and frantically tried to see the knife as the man sprang after him.

He missed grabbing the wrist but got the forearm. He gripped it with both hands, and whipping around to put his back against the other's stomach, raised his knee. He jerked the forearm hard against it as he would a length of branch for kindling.

There was a similar result—a cracking sound. The river pirate howled in pain. Lee found the knife, tore it from stubby fingers, butted hard with his backside, and jumped away. Whirling, he went at the fellow with his own knife. Down it drove—and struck, but not deeply. As the man sought to withstand him, Lee stabbed again—and again there came a pain-wracked yell.

The fellow tried to get away. He turned and took two steps, Lee after him. There was a gasp that made Lee halt, then a splash. The man had spilled overside.

One gone . . .

Turning, wet with perspiration but grimly relieved, he realized that several hand-to-hand battles were in progress along the shore side of the *Belle*. He heard Kelso's vibrant bass grunts as he tussled in the dark. There was a shout in a strange voice, another pistol explosion, thuds, scraping of feet.

Lee's corner of the keelboat seemed for the moment clear of intruders. He fumbled about for his rifle but could not find it. With the knife ready in his fist, he went noiselessly along the side aft. Slight movement a little ahead made him halt.

He stood with eyes straining but gained more from his ears reporting someone climbing aboard. Suddenly Lee located the fellow. The man sensed his charge and dodged, and Lee narrowly avoided missing him and spilling overside into the water between the barge and shore.

"That you, Baird? It's me—Rawlins. What's wrong anyway?"

Rawlins! The name sent a thrill through Lee. With a great effort he controlled his voice. "Step nearer, Rawlins."

Rawlins seemed to hesitate. "Where are you?" His groping left hand touched Lee's biceps. He moved nearer.

"I know you, Rawlins—you're Deerhide!" Lee dodged a knifeblow. Probably it saved his life, but a hot line streaked across one shoulder and a few inches of his chest. He rushed in, stabbing with his own knife.

Their weapons clacked together. Rawlins loosed a string of oaths as, evidently, he lost his. He grabbed the blade of Lee's, swung his back as Lee had to his former antagonist, and doubled forward. Lee found his chest on Rawlins's back. The fellow twisted hard and Lee's knife tore from his grasp.

Rawlins straightened and Lee spilled off him. But as Rawlins turned, Lee pounced cat-like. They slammed to the deck of the barge, the river pirate on the bottom. He was there only an instant, then twisted sideways so hard that he pitched Lee's lesser weight entirely off him.

Both came half-erect, Lee on hands and knees.

They sought to place each other. Lee charged. His onslaught knocked Rawlins's knife toward his body, and he grunted as the point of the blade must have pricked him. Now they stood grappling, straining muscles, panting hotly on each other's cheeks.

But Rawlins was more powerful. Older, more experienced, heavier, he had a wide advantage. Despite all Lee could do, the fellow was tearing from his grasp and at the same time shoving him backward, awaiting the instant he could get arm-room to drive the knife deep into Lee's chest.

A sense of desperation seized him. He was beaten. He must escape! But he could think of no way to break loose to flee.

He remembered Homer's account of river fighting. How, when a man was down, his foe sought to leap and bring down both heels in his face. Something about that vague string-like memory lead to another thought, made Lee risk his balance to thrust a leg between Rawlins's legs. He abruptly withdrew it with his foot hooked sideways.

It spilled Rawlins off balance—and the savage, killing blow he had launched missed Lee by two inches. He could feel the rush of air from the knife. It heightened fury and panic boiling within him. He shoved out—hard. It was just enough to send Rawlins reeling backward.

His balance could not be recaptured: he thudded to the deck. His shoulders and head struck a hogshead. Lee made a flying leap after and landed atop him, groping for the knife. He found it and seized the fist holding it with both hands. He lurched off, tearing the knife from the grasp of the dazed Rawlins.

There was a thud. Dazedly, Lee realized someone unsuspectedly close had swung a gun barrel at him. But it had missed and struck Rawlins's shoulder. It brought a snarl of pain from the bushwhacker. The blow momentarily prevented him from scrambling to his feet.

"You dirty riverman—!"

It was a strange voice and Lee sprang at its owner. His knife went down once, but, he feared, without much damage. Then a chance blow made him lose it, and he heard it clatter to the deck.

If he had been half in panic before, it washed over him now in a hot flood. He started to flee. But then a dark form loomed close.

"Lee!"

It was Homer Smith. There was risk in answering lest Rawlins and his confederate place Lee; still, he had to reply. "Here!" he panted, and rushed the spot where he thought Rawlins was.

They struck together. In utter amazement Lee discovered too late that they were going over the side of the keelboat. Rawlins must have stood at its edge, and Lee's onslaught carried them both over. There was an instant of falling—then the splash into

Rawlins Thudded to the Deck

the river—then its engulfing coldness.

They broke apart. Lee, an expert swimmer, bobbed up swiftly. He felt an arm drop on his head, and turned as a pair of hands groped at him. Lee knocked them away and himself searched for Rawlins's throat.

He felt it bristly under his palms. Clenching with all his muscular strength, he kept jerking his head backward and sideways to elude the hands groping for his throat. Rawlins did get hold; one wet hand slipped; he grabbed hold again.

Shouts, groans, an occasional shot and rapid scraping of boots came from the *Cumberland Belle* looming darkly near-by. The November evening was otherwise dark and still with the hush of nature in strange contrast to the savage battles in progress on the keelboat.

Treading water as Rawlins was while they gripped each other's throats, Lee had fleeting wonder that he actually was here and in such danger. Then as wire-hard fingers closed off his wind and his eyes felt bulging, he put every ounce of pressure into the squeezing of that strong, bristle-covered throat between his own hands. At the same time he gambled his draining strength to kick at Deerhide under water, and pitched his weight backward to pull the fellow below the surface.

He had got hold of the bushwhacker's throat before Rawlins had grabbed his. That was an advantage. And Lee boiled inwardly with combined desperation and hate that made him reckless, ready to spend his own life if only he took the murderer of his father with him to a watery grave.

They went under. Rawlins, unready for it, took in some water. Lee's fingers closed relentlessly tighter. The man was strangling. He was weakening.

In fierce triumph Lee strained harder—harder! He felt the hands at his own throat relax.

Instantly he had new stamina, new confidence. It was cruel to squeeze and squeeze, but Rawlins, alias the scoundrelly Deerhide, was cruel. It was a bad thing to kill a man, but Deerhide had slain many. This was necessary for Lee's own safety, and Deerhide's murders had not been necessary.

He kept treading water. Gray dots were beginning to stream crazily before his eyes. He felt far away from his own body. He felt floating in air rather than in water. Until, in vast amazement, he seemed to be lying on the *Belle's* deck.

He got his eyes open. Dawn was boldly painting the fading dark of the sky. Lee lay in a half-stupor, scarcely feeling or thinking. He slowly comprehended that the *Belle* was slipping down-river with the current. The strain and crunch of the steering oar reached him. He caught a whiff of acorn brew.

It was Homer crouching beside him. He looked exhausted and had a bloody strip of shirt wound around his head.

"Deerhide?" Lee managed weakly.

Homer's honest gray eyes narrowed. "You drowned him."

It took Lee a moment to grasp that. "Sure?"

"Saw him floating. You're pretty badly bruised up. Some cuts, too."

"We got away though?"

"We killed another, and maybe a third. There were six or seven of 'em. Kelso's all right, but John Beaver got a hard clout on the head with a gun. He's out of his senses." Homer frowned. "I don't know."

He added: "Here's some brew. You hungry?"

Homer raised him so he could sip it. The hot fluid surged down his gullet and spread warmth through him. He finished it and lay back. "Just want to sleep . . ."

It was two days before he could get around much. Muscles he had never felt before complained when he first tried walking. He was stiff and sore and the several hard bruises and minor knife cuts kept protesting with aches and pains.

John Beaver still was unable to work, though he was rational and kept insisting he would be all right. Management of the keelboat had fallen entirely on Kelso and Homer, and both were hollow-eyed and moved like men half asleep.

"We didn't dare tie up," Kelso explained wearily. "We glimpsed bushwhackers along the bank twice. And that first barge out o' Nashville—remember? We passed it grounded and two bodies on it like they's been there a couple of days. We went close, but the goods was all gone."

"There was another, too. Burned like the one you saw." Homer shook his head. "A man wants to stop and see if he can help, but it'd be foolhardy. Unless you can see half a mile in every direction. They might be waitin' behind bushes and trees. And only two of us."

Lee insisted on taking his place at the steering oar. He had eaten a huge meal of wild duck and he felt better, although still stiff. "You think it'd be safe to tie up till we're all in good shape?"

The two looked at each other. "No."

"Then one of you stay with me and the other sleep."

Homer stayed, and Kelso dropped beside the lean-to for a nap that lasted six hours. Then he joined Lee while Homer slept as if almost dead. So it went for two more days until, as they slid to a landing at the settlement of Natchez, John Beaver was stirring and able to work with them an hour or two at a time.

For five days they rested at Natchez. The news they brought of the river pirates caused little surprise among the Negro slaves working along the water front. Such reports were almost daily fare. A few sun-browned planters astride glossy horses rode to the shore and asked for news, and they too scarcely lifted their eyebrows on learning that three barges out of five had been wrecked.

"What about the war? Any news on that?" Lee asked.

"We heard General Jackson's in Mississippi Territory. He was at Fort Mims and moved on toward Pensacola. Of course, the Spanish own that," a young planter said. "But the Spaniards and the British have some understanding, and Jackson suspects the British are based at Pensacola."

"Anything from the North?"

"No-o. Things are bad, but nothing much is definite. All our campaigns seem to have accomplished nothing."

"Have the British landed to march on Washington?"

"Not that I've heard of, though it probably could be done easily enough. In spite of our gallant ships and sailors, the British have won control of the seas." The man shook his head dolefully.

The war was going badly, then. Lee hoped that General Jackson was managing to be effective against the Indian tribes fired into massacring settlers by British gold and liquor and promises to return their former hunting grounds. But it still must be almost a hopeless task Jackson faced. He would be moving steadily farther from his base of supplies, risking disease and starvation, the possible treachery of guides, and the menace of Britain's trained soldiery and navy.

He thought of Mr. Terry back in Nashville. Lee would not need to pay storage on his goods now, having killed the infamous Deerhide. It wasn't much satisfaction to avoid the storage charge, though there was some in thinking he had rid the frontier of its most lurid bushwhacker.

"That youngster killed him?" a man asked skeptically when Homer proudly told how Lee and Rawlins's struggle had ended.

"Certainly he did. I saw Deerhide floating, drowned. He had everybody fooled that he was an honest riverman. Why, he was even General Jackson's agent in charge of this keelboat!"

The planter looked more unconvinced than ever. "No seventeen-year-old, not even one of your hardy Tennesseeans, could kill Deerhide. Maybe he floated away playin' possum. Far as him being General Jackson's agent—" He started off. "I never met General Jackson, but I've heard mah kinfolk say he's surely no fool."

Homer looked angrily after him. But Lee only chuckled.

"Ready to shove off? Let's get to New Orleans and have this trip ended!"

CHAPTER TEN

CITY OF CREOLES

New Orleans!

After fifty-one days, the two-thousand-mile journey floating down-river was ended. It had begun to seem to Lee that he would always awaken to the lapping of the Mississippi against the keelboat's sides, always gaze at a low, little-changing shore line in the distance. For almost two months he had lived entirely in the open, enduring all kinds of weather and eating a diet sometimes plentiful in game but often seriously short of everything. For days he and Homer had planned their first errand ashore—to have luxurious baths, haircuts, and get their clothes laundered.

These were more easily accomplished than the sale of the cargo of the *Cumberland Belle*. Red Feather Rawlins presumably must have received full instructions for disposing of General Jackson's property in New Orleans; but Rawlins had turned out to be the notorious Deerhide and now must be dead. Kelso, veteran of nine down-river trips, remembered a firm of cotton brokers General Jackson had formerly dealt with. He and Homer and John Beaver named Lee a committee of one to call on

Boggs, Davidson & Co.; but there he learned that Jackson no longer did business with them.

"He got angry because we had to deduct brokerage, insurance, handling, warehousing and freight to England from the money due him," the junior partner of the firm told Lee frankly. "The General said we left him no profit. So, young man, he mightn't approve you trading with us. The General," he reminded, "can get angrier than any man alive."

Lee agreed that he might better dispose of the cargo elsewhere. For two days he wandered around busy New Orleans, questioning this broker and that, and finally reported to his companions.

"Seems like the best way might be to hire an auctioneer. Prices are pretty high, since not so much produce is coming down-river. That's because of the war. What do you think?"

Beaver, Kelso, and Homer voted to hire an auctioneer. And now, on a sunny, cool but not cold, winter morning, all the bales of cotton and the piles of hides and tobacco had been sold. The *Cumberland Belle* too had been sold, though for a very low price since she was worth only the timber in her.

They were in the auctioneer's office near the broad levee that banked the Mississippi. From outside sounded the bustle of Negro stevedores, with now and then a snatch of song as they wrestled huge bales down gangplanks. In the rutty street drays creaked and drivers swore at their teams of horses or oxen and there was a melange of sound from men calling to each other and moving about on their business.

"Young man," the tall, drooping-mustached auctioneer told Lee, "this is a good deal of money to take care of. And let me advise you that New Orleans is no safe town to have cash in. Our police are ineffective. There are half a dozen sluggings every night and a few stabbings and maybe a murder or two. Knockout drops may be in anything you drink."

He paused, thumbs tucked in the pockets of his flowered vest, fingertips drumming his meager stomach. "How do you propose to safeguard this money?"

Lee looked at the pile of gold coins on the desk. There was more than seven thousand dollars in all. Of that sum, eleven hundred dollars was his for the cotton and tobacco and hides that had come from the Baird farm. The remainder belonged to General Jackson. Homer, Kelso, and silent John Beaver stood near-by, counting and pocketing the wages Lee had just paid them.

He frowned. "I don't know. What can I do with it?"

"I wouldn't want to guard it for you, my young friend. Few men would. What are your plans now? Are you starting back for Tennessee?" The auctioneer shook his head gloomily. "It's dangerous—

very dangerous!"

"No, I want to join General Jackson. He's been reported near Mobile. I mean to join his army."

"Then you scarcely want to risk taking this money with you. For it's a rugged overland trip to Mobile. There are Indians on the way, and no one knows when they may take the warpath. Certainly the British seem to be trying to get them to rise up. And the whites you'll encounter—" He sighed. "No, you'd best not get yourself murdered. Assuming," he added pessimistically, "that you get out of this city alive."

Lee counted the money into a rawhide pouch. He tucked the pouch inside his shirt. "Well, thank you, Mr. Antoine, for your services. I guess we'll talk matters over among ourselves."

The four went outdoors. It was difficult even to cross the narrow, winding street to the levee because of drays and burdened stevedores milling around. Lee led the way to an oak tree from whose limbs thick gray moss hung down. He sat down in its shade, and the others followed suit.

"You going to start back for Tennessee, Kelso?" Lee asked.

Kelso nodded. "There's a party leaving in an hour. John Beaver here's coming with me."

Lee looked at Homer. "I guess I'll go too," Homer decided. "I don't like New Orleans. It's got too many people. And they're funny-looking—all Spanish or

French, or mixed. There aren't many Americans here, that's sure."

"Louisiana only became a state about two years back," Kelso said. "It used to belong to Spain, and then Napoleon got it for France. Then he sold it to the United States. But, like you say, almost everybody here is Spanish or French—or mixed blood, what they call Creole."

Lee sat thinking. The other three had decided that he should care for General Jackson's money because he had money of his own to care for. Too, they said he would be seeing the General before they did, and knew him better anyhow.

The four talked a while; then Kelso glanced at the sun. He yawned and got to his feet. "There's a few things I want to buy, and we'll be starting soon."

Homer and John Beaver also arose. Lee got to his feet, his brown brows crinkled in worry.

"You better not go in any of those fancy-lighted houses where the music and girls are, especially at night," Kelso advised.

"And I've heard that in a saloon a man might seem to become your friend, but he's only waiting to put knockout drops in your drink," Homer supplied.

"Don't get a knife stuck in your back in a dark alley," John Beaver warned.

Lee shrugged. "I certainly don't like being responsible for all this money. And as Mr. Antoine said, I can't safely take it with me to join General Jackson around Mobile."

There was silence. Kelso held out his hand. "Well, good luck, Lee."

The others also shook hands. Lee stood under the moss-hung tree and watched them pick their way among the carts as they went up the dusty street. In a moment his companions of the river trip had vanished. He never saw them again.

The bulge of the rawhide pouch felt twice as large as it actually was. Walking slowly away from the towering oak, Lee had the feeling that every Negro and white man in New Orleans was eyeing him and feeling the sharp blade of the knife in his pocket and wondering whether he could murder Lee and flee with his money.

Pshaw, it couldn't be as bad as that! Mr. Antoine, the auctioneer, seemed to be an honest man. There must be others as honest in New Orleans.

Halting, he pondered the matter. The eleven hundred dollars of his own money was all he possessed in the world. It was to provide him with support for two years, perhaps longer, while he studied law back in Nashville. That is, when he eventually got back to Nashville, which might not happen for many months. He wanted to go soldiering, and no one could foretell how long the war would last between the United States and Great Britain.

But more than for his own money, he was concerned for General Jackson's. If he should lose the General's money he never would feel entitled to hold his head up again. It was the gravest responsibility he had ever had.

His eyes narrowed, lips pursed, he tried to think. Yes! There was a good idea. He decided to act on it at once.

Going back to the auctioneer's office, he asked Mr. Antoine to suggest where he might find a room with a respectable family. He was tired from the long trip and wanted to rest up a few days in some safe shelter. He would want to see New Orleans, and too, needed to buy some better clothes for the rough army life he intended.

"There's a nice widow lady, Madame Loiret, who lives on Toulouse Street. You tell her I sent you," Mr. Antoine said. "She'll give you a clean room if she has one available, and you'll be handy to the heart of the city. Do you drink liquor, young man?" he asked.

"No, sir."

"Stick to that," Mr. Antoine advised. "You'll get in much less trouble."

Lee started for the Toulouse Street address. In half an hour he had paid for a neat and clean second floor room in the home of a Madame Loiret. It looked secure and snug, and he felt a little better for having a place he could temporarily call home.

He dared not leave the money in his room, however. There was no telling who might find and steal it. No, the safest thing was to carry it with him at all times. Lee had a good knife handy inside his trousers waistband, and he had purchased a pistol. His rifle, which was too cumbersome to carry about would mark him as a frontiersman, so he left it in his room.

There were banks in New Orleans where he could deposit his money, but how then could it be transferred to Nashville? There was no way. Folks here distrusted banks anyhow, for robberies were not uncommon and sometimes the bankers proved untrustworthy.

"If only General Jackson was coming here," Lee reflected. "Then I could just wait for him."

But the General was not expected. He was still occupied with his long campaign against the Creeks in the Mississippi Territory and would continue to be for many months to come. As for the war on the other fronts, it still seemed to be going poorly for the American side. News was scarce, and Lee was clear-sighted enough to realize that if the country's forces had scored any notable success it would have received plenty of publicity. He was discouraged at the thought of it all, and wished mightily that he might see General Jackson and persuade him to change his attitude about Lee's very real desire to get into the fight.

He overheard a man on the street gloomily remark to a companion, "I don't know what we'll do if the British decide to move against the Gulf. They can capture our whole coast and New Orleans, too." He shrugged in the expressive gesture of the Creoles.

"No trouble at all," the other man declared. "There are traitors right in this city who'll help the British!"

He also heard scattered rumors about the progress of General Jackson's campaign against the Indians. The American forces were far from their base of supplies and great difficulty was being experienced in getting sufficient food to them. The men were becoming disaffected and inclined to desert. Their ranks were being thinned by dysentery and swamp diseases, and many were suffering from wounds inflicted by Indian arrows and Indian-fired British muskets. It was even said that General Jackson himself was very ill. Lee's heart ached as he remembered how pale and infirm the General had looked when last he saw him at The Hermitage.

He strolled about the picturesque city ninety miles above the actual mouth of the Mississippi, listening and looking and learning. He couldn't decide what to do with this worrisome pouch of gold coins that made the tell-tale bulge in his shirt.

He was eager to be off to join General Jackson. However, he could hardly make the trek alone, and had not yet learned of any party setting out for

Mobile. And he couldn't help growing more and more worried about keeping his and the General's money safe!

The evening after Kelso and the others had departed, he narrowly escaped robbery and perhaps even death. A sharp-eyed, soiled-looking man in the pale blue ruffled shirt and shiny long-tailed coat had tried twice during the afternoon to strike up an acquaintance.

"Come and have a drink, friend," he had invited. "I'd like to ask you about the river above Natchez."

Lee had shaken his head and hurried on. His clothes, he knew, stamped him as a stranger, a frontiersman. He hurried on down Rampart Street and when he was swallowed in a crowd, glanced back. The fellow was sauntering in his wake.

A second time the man had accosted him. Lee sat on the grass in the little park before St. Louis Cathedral. The bulky white mason structure of the Cabildo, or government building, stood on one side of the high-spired church. The stranger came along smiling in a friendly way. "Ah, M'sieu, you like our city? Let me show you around—"

Hurriedly Lee had gotten up and walked away. But again, as he turned out of the Place d'Armes, he looked back and saw he was followed. And while he dined in a little cafe on delicious bouillabasse, a fish soup, he saw the man waiting across the street. Later, as Lee hurried around block after block searching for his rooming house, he knew he was being followed.

It was dark at the corner of Toulouse and Royal Streets. Lee stepped in an unseen puddle, gave an exclamation, and jumped to the broken board sidewalk. As he did so someone stepped toward him out of the deep shadow.

Instinctively dodging, he struck out with his left fist. There was the swishing sound of a descending knife that missed him by only a hair's breadth. Forgetting that he was close to Madame Loiret's, he ran across Toulouse and east along Royal.

Only two or three persons were in sight. Here and there saloons were lighted and from their open doorways floated talk and laughter and song. Lee, running, and glancing anxiously over his shoulder, knew that man still was after him.

His heart felt huge in his chest and was slamming like a club against his ribs. He glanced anxiously this way and that. For an instant he thought of darting into one of the saloons. But he remembered that his pursuer might have friends in any of these places who would help him drag Lee out into darkness again to murder and rob him.

He kept running, searching for some place to hide. One hand clutched the pouch of money, and he kept seeing General Jackson's thin, eagle-like face before his eyes.

Of a sudden he turned into a black alley. Halting

The Strange Man Still Followed Him

and breathing gently, though his lungs felt half exploding, he waited. He had his knife in one hand now, his pistol ready in the other.

He heard the rapidly nearing tap-tap of steps. They slowed, then stopped. There was no sound save the distant noise and music from the saloons.

Lee waited. He was tense with apprehension lest his cunning adversary manage somehow to come close without being seen or heard. Any instant he expected the cold steel of the fellow's knife to cut into his flesh.

Abruptly he sucked in his breath. His pistol jumped in his hand. There was a roar and a spear of red slashed from its muzzle. The vague black form only a few feet away was briefly illumined. There came a snarl, a flood of oaths, and the man—unhit—pounced at Lee.

In desperation, he slashed out with his knife. It caught the fellow's coat, he thought, for there was a sound of ripping cloth. The attacker swiftly retreated. Then something went *ping-g!* close to Lee's ear. It was a knife, hurled with full force at his head. It had missed by inches and driven itself into the plastered wall against which Lee stood.

He waited no longer! Taking to his heels, he raced up the inky-black alleyway. The cobblestones were huge and uneven, and he prayed that he would not stumble or twist an ankle or break a leg. But he was light-footed as a fleeing deer, and gained the next street in a matter of seconds.

Lee hesitated. The fellow undoubtedly was still after him. Where to go? Which way to Madame Loiret's, the only safety he could think of?

Somehow that pursuer knew that Lee had a fortune in gold on his person. Maybe he had watched the auction of the keelboat's cargo and seen Mr. Antoine pay Lee the proceeds. He had decided to get that gold for himself, and he was willing and eager to commit murder to do it.

There was no soldier or policeman in sight. In fact, Lee had seen very few men of either force so far in New Orleans. But he had to go somewhere!

The sweet music of an orchestra somewhere near made him glance upward. Frowning, he saw that across the street from where he stood and a little way up the block, there were bright lights. They were on the second floor of a handsome, white-surfaced building, perhaps a hotel. Evidently it was a ballroom there. Lee looked again, and saw that the street below was almost choked with carriages and fine spanking teams.

On impulse he darted across the street and hurried toward the entrance to the upstairs ballroom. Several Negro carriage men stood chatting in the light of several large whale oil lamps hung about the building entrance. Without hesitating, Lee turned in through the open doors and ran up maroon-carpeted stairs. Now and again he looked back but could not tell whether he still was being followed.

At the head of the stairway he paused. No one had noticed him but he felt suddenly conspicuous. For ladies and gentlemen in fine clothes—dozens and dozens of them—were waltzing on the gleaming ballroom floor. Other ladies and gentlemen stood talking in groups or strolling about.

The grandeur of the scene almost took his breath away. The gentlemen wore long gray or black broadcloth coats and matching trousers with straps holding them snugly around their ankles. Their shirts were of silk with many ruffles, and frothy ruffles showed at their cuffs. The ladies wore startlingly low-necked gowns of white, pink, or pale blue satin, their long skirts rustling as they danced or walked. Diamonds, emeralds and rubies flashed at their pale throats in necklaces or brooches, and other jewels sparkled in their sleek hairdresses.

Hastily moving away from the entrance, Lee took refuge behind a stand of rich green ferns. He kept watch on the entrance but did not see that sleek, oily fellow come into the ballroom. Still, he might have slipped in when Lee did not notice.

As minutes passed he began to feel more secure. Curiosity about these dozens of handsomely dressed couples made him stand watching them with round eyes and mouth slightly open. Why, there were more beautiful ladies here than he had supposed were in all Louisiana! And the jewels they wore and their rich garb must be worth a fabulous sum.

The orchestra of nearly twenty men poured forth a flood of melody for the dancers. It was fascinating to watch this colorful scene of rich people at play—laughing, smiling, chatting, bowing, dancing. Here was a different world from what Lee had ever seen before, and certainly in great contrast with keel-boating down the Mississippi!

A knot of gentlemen strolling nearer paused on the other side of the clump of ferns shielding Lee. There were four in all, but two looked as if they might be brothers. They were of wiry build, dark-skinned, and had intent, animated eyes. The shorter of the brothers interested Lee most.

"—indeed, Monsieur Lafitte," one of the other men was saying.

Lafitte . . . The name struck a responsive chord in Lee. His jaw dropped and he stared. These, then, were the famous brothers of whom he had heard—masters of a smuggling kingdom with headquarters somewhere south of New Orleans at a place called Grand Terre!

CHAPTER ELEVEN

IMPROMPTU COACHMAN

Luckily his presence behind the fern went unnoticed, for the way Lee stared would have made the Lafitte brothers and their companions think him deliberately eavesdropping to learn any secrets they might divulge.

He swallowed hard, cast quick glances around, and huddled closer under the fern's lush drooping leaves. If he were discovered it might go hard with him. The Lafittes were powerful in New Orleans and could have him dispatched swiftly at the mere crook of a finger.

The shorter brother had his back to Lee, but a side of his dark face showed. He stood talking and smiling, and Lee noted how the others, even the older, Pierre, deferred to him in their manner and speech. And there was a certain stamp of character to the man, as if he was accustomed to homage. Though slightly built, he looked hard and agile; and he was an impressive figure in his subdued but obviously rich garments and with his modulated voice and expressive gestures illustrating what he said.

Lee had heard of Jean Lafitte—as who in Louisiana had not? His name was as frequently mentioned here in New Orleans as it had been while the *Cumberland Belle* had lain tied up at Natchez. It was hard to believe that this man, evidently in his thirties and looking like a prosperous business man, doctor, or lawyer, actually was the famous Jean Lafitte, smuggler and pirate.

Pierre said something, then clapped the broad shoulder of the gray-haired, thicker-built gentleman next him as they all laughed.

" 'Twas a pretty piece of wit at your expense, Mr. Livingston," the fourth gentleman said.

"Alas, so many things prove to be at my expense. But you take these gentlemen," Mr. Livingston smiled, indicating the Lafittes, "and what would expense matter? Whether 'tis of wit or of funds?"

Lee did not catch the replies for marveling that the two brothers could thus openly attend a fashionable ball. Yet they seemed as much at home and as welcome as anyone. Couples strolling past nodded and smiled at them, and the way Jean Lafitte bowed in return seemed always to bring a light flush to the cheeks of ladies and friendly looks from their escorts. New Orleans folk seemed to respect these pirates.

It was a strange thing. Yet, according to what Lee had heard, there was reason for the friendliness of the wealthy Creoles—rich idlers and business people here in the city, many of them owners of plantations as far off as two days' ride. For these gentlemen smugglers enabled them to buy at low prices Negroes brought from far-away Africa for use as plantation slaves, and to purchase supplies of many sorts which had originated in France or in Spain.

The Lafittes were smugglers, evading United States custom laws. They were also called pirates, because, sailing the blue Gulf and the Caribbean, they preyed on the merchant vessels of Europe.

In the old days of Spanish rule over Louisiana, the government levied high duties on all imported goods. Smuggling flourished until breaking the law in this manner became generally accepted. When French ownership came, duties still were kept high and smuggling increased along with the needs of Louisiana's growing population. Now, under the United States rule, though customs duties had been lowered somewhat, the demand continued for slaves and low-priced foreign goods. Indeed, flouting the law was considered respectable, and only feeble attempts were made to enforce it.

Pierre and Jean Lafitte, hailing from Bordeaux, France, had come to New Orleans some years ago. They had opened a blacksmith shop on St. Philip Street, but gradually, in addition to their smithing, had begun to earn commissions as agents in the sale of smuggled goods. Their fortunes improved, then were threatened when bands of pirates and smugglers began to quarrel among themselves and to waylay and murder each other.

Jean Lafitte—so Lee had heard—boldly traveled the sixty miles below New Orleans to the pretty island of Grand Terre. Calling the various smuggler chiefs together, he pointed out that battles among them would weaken all until they fell easy prey to the bungling force of customs agents. By sheer weight of his personality and arguments, Lafitte had made himself king of the lawbreakers. When one smuggler captain questioned his right to rule, Lafitte had whipped out a pistol and shot the man dead. Since then, his authority undisputed, he had welded them into a single great band.

Now Grand Terre, on Barataria Bay, which in turn gave onto the sixteen hundred mile-wide Gulf of Mexico, was headquarters for all smuggling. And the Lafittes were in command, with Pierre in New Orleans representing their interests in the little blacksmithy on St. Philip Street, and Jean spending most of his time at Grand Terre. Some fifty vessels made the island their home port, their lawless motley crews and families totaling almost a thousand souls. It was the greatest organization of smugglers history had known.

To obtain goods to smuggle, the outlaws attacked vessels on the high seas. Especially bitter against Spain, the Lafitte brothers urged their ships to capture all Spanish vessels sighted. However, it was said some French merchantmen also were taken, and perhaps some British ships too.

From the great loot thus captured the Lafittes fed all Louisiana's demand for goods and slaves by means of auctions held at Grand Terre. New Orleans business men and up-country planters made the tedious journey through winding canals and swamps to these auctions. Some goods, it was said, were sold in New Orleans by certain merchants. Since the goods cost the pirates only their effort, prices were attractively low. It made up a huge volume of business, all controlled by this soft-voiced, harmless-looking man across the fern from Lee.

Suddenly he held his breath. Pierre Lafitte, excusing himself to leave, was looking straight at Lee through the lacey ferns. For an instant his blood seemed to stop coursing through his veins. But the older Lafitte did not change expression and, turning, walked off. Lee knew he had not been seen and his relief was vast.

He crouched lower, trying to make himself very small. The minutes dragged past until Mr. Livingston also departed. Then Jean Lafitte and the fourth gentleman took themselves away, and in a moment Lee saw the smuggler king bowing before a lady. She rose from her little gilded chair and they began to circle the floor in a waltz.

Glancing this way and that, Lee sought escape. But though he had come in here unhesitatingly enough it seemed to require more courage now to leave. His dress was such that anyone noticing would surely stare and perhaps stop him. Or if one of the blue-and-gold costumed attendants seized his arm, Lee would scarcely know what to say.

It was late—past midnight, he thought. The company was thinning out as couples moved away for wraps. Lee spied Jean Lafitte dancing with another lady, then lost him again. He searched through the fern for the sleek, oily-looking man who had tried to stab and rob him, but decided the fellow must not have followed him into the ballroom. Perhaps he had not seen where Lee went seeking safety. Or if he had seen him dart in here and feared to follow, he might by now have taken himself away.

Lee smoothed his unruly dark hair. Nervously moistening his lips, he watched for a chance to leave. When almost everyone still present was on the glistening dance floor he hesitantly stole from behind his green protection. Shoulders back, trying to keep a casual look on his face, he strolled toward the entrance.

Two lackeys at the top of the staircase in bulky powdered wigs and rich uniforms spied him approaching. Amazed, they blinked in unison, as if they had rehearsed it. Both glanced away, then looked back quickly, scowling. Simultaneously they started for Lee.

He rushed between them. Just as the two lackeys closed from opposite sides of the stairway, Lee went scuttling down the richly carpeted stairs he had mounted an hour or more ago.

"Stop!"

"Come back here!"

The lackeys' shouts attracted notice from a few people standing near. Glancing back, Lee saw the pair hurrying after him. The sight started a panicky tickling in his stomach that made him go faster. Jumping two and three stairs at a time, he ran out the door into Royal Street.

Two coachmen stood talking in the oil-lamp-lighted entrance. They looked up as Lee dashed past them, heading for the nearest protective darkness. The lackeys, following him out on the plank sidewalk, glanced up and down the street.

"Did you see a ruffian just run out?" one asked.

A coachman nodded. "He went that way. Was he a thief?"

"Probably," the other lackey growled. "Else what would a fellow of his stripe be doing at a ball?"

"But I haven't heard of anything stolen, Francois," his companion remembered. "Perhaps the lout was merely curious and ventured a look at his betters enjoying themselves."

The two slowly disappeared back up the stairs, and Lee heaved a sigh. He kept watching the coachmen while he mopped his forehead with his sleeve. They stared directly at him from some forty feet distant; but because of the dark neither could see him, he knew. After a moment they seemed to decide the fugitive must by now be out of reach.

It was a passageway between two buildings in which Lee stood. When his excited breathing had calmed, he peered cautiously up and down for that murderous fellow who had been after him. There was no sign of the man, though he might be lurking, as Lee was, in one of the many dark niches.

He scarcely knew whether to be off in search of Madame Loiret's or to stay here longer. But he had a feeling his assailant still lurked about, waiting. It warned him against walking boldly along the street.

While he tried to decide what to do and which way Madame Loiret's must lie, Lee felt of the heavy pouch full of gold coins that bulged his shirt. Then his roving gaze fixed on Jean and Pierre Lafitte emerging from the ballroom entrance. Both now wore graceful black capes with red silk linings showing as the wind curled back their corners. Pierre asked a doorman who had appeared to summon their carriage.

"Quickly, my man!" Jean Lafitte urged.

The doorman trotted down a line of carriages awaiting their owners. He returned and trotted similarly along the sidewalk past Lee. At last there came a rattle of hoofs that proved the Lafittes' carriage had been found. The doorman trotted back to the ballroom entrance; then Lee saw the smart turn-out rolling after.

An impulse gripped him. After a swift glance up and down the sidewalk he ran out between two waiting carriages. As Jean Lafitte's rolled past, Lee darted around its high rear wheel and running after it, groped for a means of hoisting himself onto its protruding springs.

By grasping the top edge of the back seat he was able to jump and get his feet on the exposed rear axle. Then Lee crouched, half-seated, on one spring. The carriage halted abruptly and he made himself as small as possible lest waiting coachmen see him.

But no one marked his presence. In a moment the two Lafittes had climbed aboard and the driver was starting his spanking team of black horses. While Lee clung to his precarious spring-seat, the equipage jolted over the cobblestones.

His eyes glinted. Staring back, he had glimpsed a dark form in a doorway. It was the fellow who had sought to murder him and, he supposed, rob him. So his premonition of danger had been right!

He began to feel better, for he must be safe now. If he could recognize Toulouse Street, he meant to jump off the carriage and hurry to Madame Loiret's. And certainly the first thing tomorrow he must find someone with whom to leave this money!

The corners passing, however, looked unfamiliar in the dark. A few minutes later the carriage drew to a stop before a one-story cottage-type building. A whale oil street lamp was near but Lee kept concealed while the two Lafittes bade their coachman good-night and crossed the sidewalk. In response to their knock the cottage door opened and the brothers vanished within.

What happened next whisked Lee's breath away. A low whistle sounded, and instantly men appeared out of the dark from all directions.

One glance at the pair not twelve feet from him on the sidewalk told Lee by their uniforms and weapons that they were soldiers. The first low-toned command proved it.

"Here, what's this? Who are you?" the Lafitte coachman demanded.

"Stay where you are. We're United States soldiers!"

The coachman ejaculated an oath. There was a rustle of footfalls as eight or ten men joined their heavy-set leader on the sidewalk before the cottage. There followed a low-toned parley which Lee could not catch. The door knocker sounded again, and the officer of the detail cried, "Open in the name of Governor Claiborne!"

The door did swing open, and Jean Lafitte stood there outlined.

"I have a warrant for the arrest of one Pierre Lafitte of this address," the officer announced. "I demand his surrender!"

Lafitte seemed surprised. He glanced over his shoulder. "Yes," he said. "Will you step in?"

The officer and two soldiers entered. There was brief talk. "–house is surrounded," Lee caught.

Some two minutes dragged past. Then Pierre Lafitte, again wearing his dark cape and silky hat, emerged with the officer. The soldiers followed and the door closed after them.

"Is it necessary to walk?" Pierre asked. "We could use the carriage."

"Can I drive you, sir?" The coachman climbed down to the sidewalk and opened the door.

"Lieutenant," one of the officer's aides spoke up, "the other warrant is for Paul LeFevre. I believe this driver is he."

As the coachman stepped back he was seized. "Are you Paul LeFevre?" the officer demanded.

The coachman struggled until Lafitte told him to surrender. "But wh-what have I done?"

"You are under arrest for smuggling. Now let's be off!"

The several other soldiers guarding the cottage were called and Pierre Lafitte and Paul LeFevre were marched away. Their footfalls echoed hollowly down the street, thinning until they were gone.

Lee stood amazed. It seemed a miracle that he had crouched here entirely unnoticed. Of course, if arrested he could have told his story easily enough. But would it have been as easy to convince the Lafittes as the soldiers?

He stepped to the sidewalk and stood thinking.

At last he turned to renew his search for Madame Loiret's. He had had enough excitement for one night, and—

He heard a latch click. The Lafitte cottage door opened and Jean emerged. "Quick, Paul," he called. "On your box!"

Looking around, Lee realized that Lafitte had spoken to him. He had mistaken Lee for the coachman who had been arrested.

Lafitte gave Lee a little shove as he crossed the walk and jumped into the coach. "Hurry, Paul!" He slammed the door. "To Mr. Livingston's!"

With a great effort, Lee mastered his surprise. He could run and get away . . . a wild impulse came and he obeyed it.

"Yes, sir!" Climbing to the coach seat he took the reins wrapped around the socketed whip. "Mr. Livingston's?" he queried. "I—er, don't seem to remember—"

"You've been there," Lafitte returned impatiently. "Turn right at this corner for two squares, then left for half a square. The big white mansion—you'll recognize it. And hurry. They've arrested Pierre. But I mean to get him out of that dirty, wet Cabildo cell as quickly as I can!"

Lee slacked the reins, and the black horses strained to their harness. The carriage rolled away from the modest cottage which was the New Orleans headquarters of the pirate brothers Lafitte.

CHAPTER TWELVE

TAVERN FRIENDS

Lee found the way easily enough but he was still rather dazed by his own boldness when he halted the team in front of Mr. Livingston's white pillared mansion. It stood in a large yard amid flowers, shrubs, and graceful live oak trees, the whole enclosed by a high, lacey fence of wrought iron. There was no light showing, and indeed the coach occupants seemed the only persons awake in this vicinity.

"Wait, Paul." Jean Lafitte sprang out and hurried to the gate. He got it open and went up the veranda steps, and a moment later was thumping the heavy brass knocker. Impatiently he struck it again, waited, then sounded it once more.

Presently through the glass panels beside the door and the fanlight above it a yellow light showed. Someone cautiously unlocked the door and opened it a crack.

"What dat?" Lee heard the Negro butler demand.

"Mr. Lafitte. Tell Mr. Livingston I must see him at once!"

The servitor admitted Lafitte. Watching from the sidewalk, Lee saw a light enter a study off the front hall and knew that Lafitte was impatiently waiting there. Another light appeared upstairs, and in a few moments Lee could tell that Mr. Livingston had descended to see his visitor.

Lee was wondering whether to wait for Lafitte to return or take to his heels. He had about decided it would be most sensible to depart when the front door opened and the Negro butler came out on the porch and seemed to be peering for him.

"Is Mr. Livingston at home?" Lee asked, just to make talk, and walked inside the gate and to the lower veranda step.

The Negro descended and stood near holding his lamp. "Land o' Canaan, dat man in big hurry! Can't he wait things till mawnin'?"

"Well, no, I guess not. He wants Mr. Livingston's advice in an important matter."

The other rubbed one eye sleepily. He studied Lee in the lamplight. "He say his name Lafitte, or somepin'. Dat ain't gwine be dat smuggler-man, is it?"

"Yes, that's Jean Lafitte. You know, there are two brothers. The other was arrested tonight by soldiers for Governor Claiborne," Lee explained. "I don't know what Mr. Livingston has to do with it, though. What is his profession?"

The Negro stared at Lee as if his question was silly. "Den dat man is de smuggler! Yo'all don't know who Massa Livingston is?" He drew himself up. "Massa Livingston, he de biggest lawyer in dis heah New Orleans. Dat all he is. He just de bigges' and mos' important man, almost, 'side Governor Claiborne."

"A lawyer?"

"You must be a stranger, boy, if yo'all don't know dat. Ev'body know Massa Livingston. He big lawyer in New York—dat somewhere hunnerds miles off where Yankees live," he explained. "Massa Livingston was great big lawyer, and he like it fine. But he 'cide he goin' to new country. So he come down heah where lawyers is needed and he do fine. It cost a heap o' money to hire him to git folks out o' trouble—yes, sah, a heap o' money!"

Lee was struck by a thought. "Then he's a very respected gentleman, I suppose? Hardly anyone more honest in all Louisiana?"

"Yes, sah! He could be Governor if he want. He strictly hones', all right, and he mighty prom'nent. Why, Massa Livingston—"

A call came from within the house. "Yes, sah! Comin'!" The Negro turned and shuffled his ragged slippers up the steps. As Lee watched, he closed the front door and went about the service for which he had been summoned.

Lee began to pace up and down. He was mulling over a thought which had come to him—an inspiration, perhaps it was. His hand went to the bulge in his shirt that was the hard pouch of gold coins, the large sum belonging to General Andrew Jackson and all the wealth Lee himself possessed in the world.

If Mr. Livingston was a prominent attorney—and no doubt, as the Negro had declared, he was—then Jean Lafitte must have came to request his legal services in getting his brother Pierre out of a cell in the Cabildo, the bulky white government building beside St. Louis Cathedral on the Place D'Armes. It was logical that Lafitte, with great wealth from smuggling and piracy at his command, would seek to hire the best lawyer in New Orleans.

If Mr. Livingston was the best lawyer, he must be reliable and honest. Lee went to rub the horses' soft muzzles while he thought it over again. Nodding, he turned and walked quickly down the block until he could pause in deep shadow and be certain that he was in no way visible from where the carriage waited.

He had not long to stand there. Watching the mansion door, he saw it open and saw Lafitte and Mr. Livingston stand talking against the lighted interior. The lawyer remained with his Negro butler at his elbow while Lafitte moved in his quick, nimble way down the steps and out to the carriage. The mansion door closed.

"Paul!" Lee heard Lafitte call. "Home, now."

He opened the carriage door and was about to enter when lack of response made him hesitate. Straightening, he stepped back to look up at the coachman's box. Lee heard his exclamation of annoyance and watched as Lafitte turned and stared up and down the street.

"Paul!" he called louder. "You rascal, hurry!"

Lee waited. Lafitte was becoming irritated, he could tell by the sound of his voice as the man tried again to summon his driver. Then he gave a peculiar high, wailing whistle. He waited, but got no response.

Of a sudden Jean Lafitte slammed the carriage door in a way that proved he was angry. He stalked to the fore part of the carriage, reached for the iron rung, and hoisted himself to the driver's seat. Next moment the horses obediently tugged forward and the equipage rolled down the street.

When it had turned a corner, Lee walked rapidly back to the high wrought-iron gate. Entering, he mounted the veranda and after brief hesitation, thumped the heavy knocker. The glass panels indicated that the Negro had not yet gone upstairs with his lamp, and it was only a matter of seconds before he opened the door.

"Mah goodness, Mistah Lafitte–" He broke off, recognizing Lee. "What yo'all want?" he demanded harshly.

"I have to see Mr. Livingston. It's important or I wouldn't bother him. Please call him!"

The Negro stared. He shifted his oil lamp to his other hand and scratched his head. Blinking, he

"Hurry, You Rascal," Called Lafitte

peered at Lee. "This heah ain't no trick? Dat man you was with, he ain't set you to no smugglin'?"

"No indeed. This is serious," Lee urged. "Please call him, will you?"

The other sighed. But he gestured for Lee to enter, lighted a lamp on a hallway table, then indicating that Lee should wait, laboriously climbed the handsome white-and-mahogany staircase.

In a moment Mr. Livingston followed him down. He was in ruffled shirt and trousers and looked annoyed. "Is this he?" he asked, staring at Lee.

"Sir, may I see you alone? I'm sorry to bother you at this hour, but—"

"Very well. The study, Ned." They followed the Negro into the book-lined room in which the lawyer and Jean Lafitte had talked a few minutes earlier. Mr. Livingston waved Lee to a chair and took another behind a table on which were piled several bulky law books and a variety of papers.

Lee waited until Ned had withdrawn and, still eyeing Lee suspiciously, closed sliding doors. Then he opened his shirt and drew out the pouch. He let it drop on the table so as to give off a jingle of coins.

"Sir, my name is Lee Baird. I'm from Nashville, and recently came to New Orleans on a keelboat. I don't know anyone here and my companions have started back to Nashville. I've got a good deal of money and no safe place to leave it. I thought perhaps you would take care of it for me."

Mr. Livingston was a handsome man of forty-odd years. He studied Lee with a puzzled half-smile. He looked at the pouch. "How much money do you have?"

"More than seven thousand dollars in gold. There's been a man after me all afternoon and evening, and faith, I was all but murdered for it."

"Your costume, of course, indicates that you are not a New Orleans resident. Every footpad guesses at once that you came down-river and therefore must have the wages you were paid, at least. But —do I know you?" he added.

"No, sir. But I was at the ball tonight, hiding behind a large fern. I'd run in there to get away from the man who was after me," he explained. "I didn't mean to eavesdrop, sir—I was only hiding. But I did hear some of your talk with the Lafitte brothers and another gentleman. Then—"

Lee recounted how he had escaped clinging to the Lafitte coach and how Jean Lafitte had mistaken him for the coachman, Paul LeFevre, after Paul had been arrested with Pierre. "I talked with your Negro," he explained, "and it struck me that you are an honest man and perhaps would be willing to keep my money for me. I know this is very unusual," he added quickly as Mr. Livingston started to object, "but where am I to go? What can I do with the money? And I'm not starting back to Tennessee."

"No? What is your plan?"

"To join General Jackson if I can. You see, most of this sum is his. But it wouldn't be safe to carry it—"

"Most of this money is General Jackson's? How is that?"

Lee explained how the keelboat had been built to carry the General's goods and how he had paid freight for his own produce by working on the craft. He told how Red Feather Rawlins had turned out to be Deerhide and about the desperate fight that night Deerhide's men attacked.

When he finished, Mr. Livingston's surprise was apparent. He sat drumming his fingers on the table. "And you say some eleven hundred dollars is yours, and the remainder is the property of Andrew Jackson?"

"Yes, sir, it is. Will you keep it safe for me?" Lee begged. "I can't tell how long it will be, but no longer than necessary. Should General Jackson ever come to New Orleans, the money could be paid him. He trusted us all on the keelboat, sir, and now I'm left with this gold. He's been very good to me and he's my friend and—"

He saw that further pleading would be ineffective. Mr. Livingston was thinking it over. He asked various questions concerning Lee's father, Nashville, the shooting of General Jackson by Colonel Thomas Benton and his brother. At last Lee knew by his expression that the favor asked would be granted, for Mr. Livingston was convinced of the truth of all Lee had said.

"I am not a bank, you understand. I cannot assume responsibility for your money as a bank would. But I will promise to guard it as carefully as I guard my own funds. I shall be glad to do you and General Jackson this small service."

"Thank you, Mr. Livingston! You will wish to count the money." Lee handed him the pouch.

He watched while Mr. Livingston poured the shiny gold coins onto the table and carefully counted them in little stacks. "Seven thousand three hundred and seventy dollars? That's correct, then." He produced a quill pen, ink and paper, and wrote a brief receipt.

"I suggest you keep that in a safe place on your person," the lawyer said.

"Yes, sir. I'll hide it in my boot." Lee rose. "Mr. Livingston, I'm sorry to have kept you up so late. And I do thank you, sir, for your kindness."

The other escorted him to the door, and Lee noted the increased respect Ned, the Negro, showed him on seeing how his master now treated the caller.

"I'll return for the money as soon as I can, else General Jackson will come for it. Thank you again, Mr. Livingston!"

He was outside, going down the veranda steps. On the sidewalk Lee stopped and gave a sigh of relief. Phew! That had been a fortunate thought, to ask Mr. Livingston to hold the money for him. And he liked Mr. Livingston's manner and the shrewd way he questioned Lee to be certain he was being told a true account. Yes, his money and General Jackson's was safe now—of that he felt certain. It was a great load off his mind.

Going along the street, Lee found himself whistling. Certainly he felt much better than he had an hour ago! He chuckled as he remembered Jean Lafitte having to drive himself home and doubtless cursing Paul LeFevre for having deserted him. No doubt when Lafitte reached his stable he would have to unhitch the horses, put them in stalls, feed them and perhaps even rub them down—quite an unusual task for the meticulously dressed smuggler!

Reading weathered street signs at corners, Lee was having difficulty finding Toulouse Street. When he did find Madame Loiret's, perhaps he would have trouble persuading the little French woman to admit him because of the lateness of the hour. However, first he must locate Toulouse, and in this jumble of narrow streets with lacey wrought-iron balconies seeming almost to touch in some places, a fellow could stay lost for a month!

The lights of a corner drinking place attracted him. He hadn't the treasure in gold on him now, so why not inquire there for street directions? No one could steal from him, save the few coins Lee had kept for his immediate expenses.

Caution, however, prompted him to sit down on the sidewalk edge, remove one boot, and draw out its insole. Lee folded the receipt Mr. Livingston had given him and placed it in the heel. Then he moistened the gummed insole, put it back, and carefully drew on his boot. Rising, he put all his weight on that foot to press the insole and seal it.

He raked work-hardened fingers through his hair, then set out for the tavern and boldly pushed aside the swinging doors to enter.

It was a tiny place with little tables and a sawdust-covered floor. Three men were singing rather sweetly at one table. At another a man alone was slumped over on his arms, snoring. A waiter in a soiled apron leaned against the little bar, a bored look on his face as if he wished closing time would hasten.

Lee crossed to ask the waiter his way to Toulouse Street. One of the singers overheard. He was a short, stocky, very black-haired man in a seafaring cap and red-and-black striped jersey from the top of which chest hair showed like a tuft of mattress.

"Toulouse? Right around the corner, friend," he said cheerily. Then cocked his head. "Do you sing?"

"Why—yes, I think so."

"He sings!" The sailor gave the news to his companions, one an evil-looking one-eyed individual also in sailor garb, the other a sleek little man in city dress. "He drinks too, I'll wager! Henri, something for our young friend. A beer? Liquor? Burgundy?" He gestured. "Anything—but quick, Henri!"

"Some wine, thank you," Lee said. He knew little of drink but did know that wine was weakest save beer. Feeling eager for comradeship, and having no worry now about the money, he thought he might as well have some enjoyment before going off to bed.

"Sit down! What shall we sing? Come, you also," the sailor called to another customer who had entered. But that man shook his head and dropped into a chair in front of the place, his back turned.

The waiter served Lee a glass of red wine. "To your next voyage, Captain You!" one of Lee's companions toasted.

"To a profitable voyage! As profitable as today's slave auction, eh, Dominique?" added another.

The sailor, Lee gathered, was Captain Dominique You. "There was a slave auction?" he asked when he had sipped a little wine to be sociable. "Faith, I've never seen one."

"You will. Zey are frequent," the jovial, hairy Captain said with another expressive gesture. "A fine African, excellent for ze plantation, only two hundred dollars. But if brought to Louisiana by traders, do you know how much is ze charge? Four hundred dollars!"

"Much cheaper to buy from you, Captain You," the sleek city man purred.

"Certainly! And ze good Negroes only I offer.

You weesh for a slave?"

"No," Lee returned. "I have no money. I don't think I'd want to own one anyway."

"No monee? Too bad." Captain You shrugged. "Well," he said, sipping his wine again and waving to the others to follow suit. "Now we sing, no? Let me see—First, the song of the Caribbean when she ees so blue and so fair. You know? Ze first line, 'On ze blue Caribbean we sail, ho-ho ze breeze, ho-ho ze breeze . . ."

There was a strange roaring in Lee's ears. He shook his head to drive it away but it only came louder. It swelled like rising thunder, seeming to pound from eardrum to eardrum. He was suddenly dizzy too. The little tavern was going around . . . around. That man who had entered last seemed to be standing over Lee, an evil smirk on his face.

He realized vaguely that he was lying on the floor. That Captain Dominique You and the latest arrival stood over him grinning widely while they watched him. They looked far, far above . . .

Too late Lee understood. His wine had been drugged and he was the victim of unscrupulous men.

CHAPTER THIRTEEN

WHEELSMAN FOR LAFITTE

It was fall again.

The change of seasons meant little in the broad expanse of the Caribbean, merely that winds became gustier and occasionally threatened hurricane fury. But there were no trees dropping red-tinted leaves as there had been in Tennessee.

Lee Baird turned the spokes of the steering wheel and the brig *Cartagena* filled her sails and dipped her bow deeper in the sunny blue water off the north coast of Cuba. The creak of her masts, the grunt of straining ropes, and the rumble of waves peeled aside by her bow told that all was well aboard. As her yards eased off, Lee turned the wheel again, and again the pirate vessel gave the swift response that proved her faster than any of the foreign merchantmen on which she preyed.

Automatically guiding Captain Jean Lafitte's flagship, Lee noted the *Santa,* with Captain Dominique You, holding steady off the port bow. He was thinking, not of Lafitte or the hairy Captain You, but of all that had happened to him this past year.

It scarcely seemed a year since he had abandoned his father's farm after Deerhide's midnight assault.

In a way, though, it seemed longer since Lee had worked in Mr. Roston's livery barn, visited General Jackson at The Hermitage, and started down-river on the *Cumberland Belle.*

As skillfully he kept the brig on her course, he could scarcely believe that for ten months he had actually been a sailor aboard a pirate ship.

Lee shook his head. But for Jean Lafitte, he would have been on the ocean bottom instead of afloat!

The night Dominique You and his tavern companions had drugged Lee's wine they had supposed he still had the pouch of gold coins on his person. The footpad who had earlier tried to murder Lee had glimpsed him entering the tavern, and following, had signaled You that here was their quarry.

He regained his senses dismally sick and a captive in a shack at Grand Terre. He scarcely remembered being dragged from the shack and hustled aboard the *Santa* to be at once locked in a dark, damp, smelly dungeon somewhere in her hold. He was too ill to notice the vessel putting to sea—but if he had been ill before, the slow swell of the Gulf trebled it.

On the fourth day he felt a little better. He could sip the water placed inside his dark four foot square prison. It was the afternoon of that day as Lee lay slumped almost exhausted, that the door bolts thumped back. He raised himself expectantly.

Two evil-looking sailors thrust the door aside.

Captain You stared down at Lee, a sneer curling his upper lip. He was no gay tavern singer now, but a cruel tyrant with a cunning, heartless look on his knife-scarred face. "You tell where ees the money."

"But I haven't got it! I haven't got it!"

The unemotional eyes studied Lee's haggard countenance. Captain You shrugged. At his curt order, the two husky sailors dragged Lee out of the cell and two flights up on deck. For several minutes the brilliant sun blinded him; then, glancing around, he felt his heart turning to stone.

That plank laid over the *Santa's* rail . . .

He knew what it was for. He could tell by the cold, yet slightly curious looks of hard-faced pirates loitering about the deck of the vessel anchored off some lonely island. They watched stonily as Captain You snarled a final time, "Thees money! You will now geev to me?"

"But I haven't got it! I can prove I haven't, that I gave it to—"

Dominique You kicked him viciously. His snarled order made the two sailor-guards quickly bind Lee's wrists behind him. Despite his struggles and protests a soiled bandana was tied over his eyes. The sailors seized him under the arms, lifted him, and left him wavering weakly on the end of the plank laid from a keg over the rail.

Lee knew then that he was doomed. His knees shook, and perspiration drenched him. His heart thumped club-like in his chest.

Captain You loosed a string of angry shouts. "Make heem go forward!"

A cutlass-point pricked Lee's thigh. Reacting, he impulsively stepped forward. Again that sharp jab, and again he moved. Now, able to see nothing, something told him that he was at the vessel's rail. After two or three more steps the plank would abruptly end. He would go hurtling down into the water.

A shout came from somewhere below him. He did not catch what was said. It was not from the *Santa,* though the voice seemed vaguely familiar. In response, Captain You grumbled something. Lee felt the cutlass blade pressed across his knees in front, and there was a gruff command from the pirate holding it. "Stand!"

A bustle rose alongside the *Santa.* Above the loud pounding of his heart Lee gradually realized that those sounds meant someone was coming aboard. Wild hope soared in him . . . until he recognized the soft but stern tones of Jean Lafitte, and knew that nothing good could come of the pirate king's arrival. For Lafitte must believe in forcing unwanted men—yes, and perhaps women and children—to walk the plank overside to their death.

Still, it was a moment's reprieve. Lee prayed frantically for some helpful development.

A low-voiced parley went on a few yards away. He could not hear what the men were saying. Lee could scarcely credit his great fortune when the cutlass tapped his knees and he was ordered to step back. He obeyed. The powerful hands that had lifted him up on the plank now eased him down to the deck. The blindfold was removed. He found slight, shrewd Jean Lafitte standing close in front of him. Beside Lafitte, Captain You stood scowling.

There was a moment's silence. "If you have the gold which Captain You desires, is it not sensible to give it to him and save your life?" Lafitte suggested.

"But sir, I don't have it! I—I left it with Mr. Livingston because I was afraid of being robbed!"

Lafitte glanced at You. "You left it with—"

"Yes, sir, I did! Faith, I've a receipt to prove it! I left it with him the night your brother was arrested. The night you mistook me for your coachman—"

Anxiously, pleadingly, Lee poured out his story. At first he could detect no sign of yielding in Lafitte's face and the stocky Captain You looked more and more surly.

But gradually, as Lee detailed his experience hiding behind the fern at that fashionable ball, concealing himself on the back of the Lafitte carriage, and boldly playing coachman, Jean Lafitte seemed to soften. And Lee saw that his story squared perfectly with what the pirate king knew.

"Hm. The receipt?"

"Sir, can I have my hands free? 'Tis in my left boot!"

Lee Pleadingly Poured Out His Story

Captain You gestured an order. Lee was seized and unceremoniously dropped on the deck. Two husky rascals of the crew worked his boot off. At Lee's direction one probed with his knife, ripped out the inner sole and produced the folded paper. It was handed to Jean Lafitte, who read it and showed it to Captain You.

" 'Tis indeed Mr. Livingston's signature." He began to smile broadly; then a laugh started in his throat and grew until he was slapping his thigh. "Ah, Dominique! To let a callow Tennessee lad cheat you of seven thousand dollars!"

The other growled oaths and glared. "Why you not say?" he demanded of Lee.

"I—you didn't give me a chance. I'd have told you if you had."

Lafitte handed the receipt back to Lee. His eyes still twinkled. "Now what, Dominique?"

"I keel thees boy! He does not geev me the gold. I do not want his carcass on my ship!"

Lafitte plucked his lieutenant's sleeve and drew him aside. They spoke in low tones. Lafitte strolled back.

"You may live if you join my crew. We have no room for idlers."

Lee thought fast. It came to the very tip of his tongue to defy him, to refuse to become a pirate. Certainly he had no taste for such an occupation. He was no lawbreaker!

Still, life was precious. He would be a fool stubbornly to refuse this chance to live. There was always hope that escape might be possible . . . yes, to refuse would be suicide. There was no real choice: he wanted to live!

He met Jean Lafitte's steady eyes. "I agree."

Freed, he had been brought in a whaleboat to the *Cartagena*. For a while he was guarded on her broad, clean deck. Later, when the vessel was under way, Jean Lafitte beckoned him to follow and led the way to his cabin.

It was in the stern of the brig just above the grinding rudder post. It was a cozy cabin of fair size but crowded with furniture and weapons and maps and books. Lafitte dropped into his chair before a littered table.

"You are prepared to serve me faithfully? Anything less," he warned, "will mean your death."

Lee bit his lip. "I don't want to join you," he said slowly. "But I do want to live. I don't want to be an outlaw, a smuggler, and pirate. With a price on my head!" he ended bitterly.

Jean Lafitte looked anything but an outlaw, smuggler, or pirate. He had the quiet appearance and manner of a respectable man of trade. At Lee's outburst his eyes flashed briefly; then he smiled.

"Your name is Lee Baird?" At Lee's nod he went on as if explaining something to a small boy who could comprehend only simple terms. "Some call me a smuggler and pirate. I see it differently. Do not Louisiana folk want Negro slaves at low prices? And silks, and all manner of supplies? If I did not furnish them, someone else would. Your fine citizens of New Orleans agree that the customs levies are outrageously high. So I am but a merchant selling his wares to the market that wants them.

"I, like you, am an American," he said. "Yes—" as Lee stifled an exclamation—"and when our customs laws are changed, as some time they must be, I shall lose my business. Is it not better for this business to be well organized under me than to have forty or fifty vessels' crews fighting each other and preying on anything afloat?

"Remember," he went on softly, "I sail under letters of marque. These letters, if you do not understand, authorize me to capture any vessels of Spain. They are issued by the Republic of Cartagena, after which this ship is named. I am in the service of Cartagena, and Cartagena is at war with Spain. It is the same as Americans capturing British merchantmen because their countries are at war. Would that be piracy?"

He let that sink in. "I do not like killing people. My orders are to set ashore the crews of captured vessels, where that is possible. Or to put them adrift with provisions. But the goods of my enemies I capture. They are my prize."

He paused. "Now, Lee Baird, you are young. Your

life is before you. You can serve in my crew, or—" He shrugged. "I have no space aboard for anyone who will not serve."

Lee stood silent for a moment, trying to think what he could reply. "As an American," he said slowly, "I am at war with Britain and only Britain. I want to join General Jackson and eventually go back to Nashville."

"You would fight if we were attacked?"

"Yes-s. For defense."

Jean Lafitte seemed slightly amused with this tall, lanky youth before him—amused by Lee's doggedness in the face of his danger. There was even some hint of liking in his keen, dark eyes. "Doubtless you could make yourself useful as a lookout—or a wheelsman."

Lee was not sure what this entailed. But he nodded. "Yes, sir. I'll do the best I can."

And so it was. Months had elapsed and now he was a proficient wheelsman. The operation of the brig was as orderly as that of a man-o'-war, with assignments regularly given out and watches strictly observed. Lee was on duty four hours, off four hours, and free within the confines of the vessel whenever she lay anchored.

They had taken seven prizes during his three voyages—two vessels during this last month. One, loaded with gaunt, terrified Negroes, had been a slave frigate from the Gold Coast of Africa. She had been heading for Havana to sell the miserable human cargo in her foul 'tween decks.

When the two vessels were grappled together and the *Cartagena's* boarding party scrambled like monkeys over the rails bumping and grinding, the stench from the Spanish ship wafted to Lee at the wheel. It was the smell of filth from human beings ill-treated and unwashed and kept in chains.

The Spanish crew had been set adrift. They would be picked up in a day or two, likely. A prize crew from the *Cartagena* went aboard the *Alfonso*. On Lafitte's order the Negroes were given fresh air, water, and food. They were brought on deck in groups for exercise, and their piteous fright amid men they had never beheld, in a clime they had never seen, touched Lee's heart. He was glad that Lafitte had captured them from the brutal Spaniards, for at least the poor wretches could expect better treatment from then on.

In Cuba they would have brought from a hundred to two hundred fifty dollars each, depending on whether they were males capable of hard plantation labor or females useful in kitchen or housework, or children who could grow up to be laborers. The Spaniards had planned to auction them in Cuba, whence buyers would transport many to the United States for re-sale at double the prices.

The *Alfonso* had sailed for Grand Terre. The other recent prize, a merchantman out of Cadiz, had been laden with silks, spices, and machinery. A prize crew from the *Cartagena* had sailed her also for Grand Terre.

The *Santa* too had captured a slaver and sent her home. Now the two pirate vessels were sailing together. It had been a profitable voyage, and Lee, after ten months with Jean Lafitte, had seen and experienced the business of piracy.

It seemed, as Lafitte had said, to be only privateering when, under internationally recognized letters of marque, he captured the vessels of Spain. But piracy came in when an occasional French slaver or merchant ship, and perhaps one now and then owned by the British, were taken. Lee thought Lafitte did not approve of these captures but permitted them to avoid rebellion by his crew.

Slowly he had come to admire Jean Lafitte. According to the man's own lights he was no scoundrel. He admitted evading United States customs laws but held it a small sin because all Louisianians considered the customs duties unreasonable. Lafitte declared this lawbreaking was outweighed by the service he rendered cotton and rice planters by bringing them Negro slaves at low prices.

Somehow Lee respected him. He was not cruel as pirates generally were said to be cruel. He always gave merchant vessels opportunity to surrender, usually signaling them who he was and demanding that they yield. If they resisted, his battle strategy was so deft that boarding was brief and with few casualties.

Lee stood turning the *Cartagena's* wheel to hold her on course. About her sunny deck sailors sat or stood in twos and threes. Some were at work splicing ropes or coiling them, others holystoning the deck, others tarring cracks in the towering masts. A few loitered at the rails talking and smoking.

A step sounded behind Lee. It was Jean Lafitte, neatly dressed as always, a quiet business man save for the cutlass and pistol thrust inside the sash around his waist under the long broadcloth coat.

He spoke briefly with Quartermaster Scovelli behind Lee. Scovelli gave an ejaculation. "But, sir—"

"A hurricane might cost us our vessel and our lives. Cheaper to run for it, Scovelli. And we've had a good voyage. Too, we've given away too many of our crew, and we're short on provisions."

The quartermaster hesitated. Lee knew he was scowling. "Aye aye, sir."

Lafitte strolled away. Catching Lee's eye, he nodded and gave his half-smile. "Good morning."

"Morning, sir."

The pirate king paused. "Do you, by chance, know sums? Can you read and write?"

"Yes, sir. I figure fairly well and read and write readily."

Lafitte pondered. "No doubt you plan, at the first opportunity, to desert me?"

"This is my third voyage, Captain Lafitte."

"Yes—because you did not find the opportunity to get back to New Orleans. Is that not so?"

It was, of course. Lee did not want to continue this life. Despite Jean Lafitte's arguments and explanations and the grudging respect Lee held for him, smuggling still seemed to him wrong, and he was by no means certain it was right to seize unarmed merchant vessels of any nation.

"When we make Grand Terre," Lafitte said, "I shall want your reading and figuring. You will work on my accounts."

He walked away. Lee looked after him, surprised. Yet, perhaps book-work on shore would provide him an opportunity to quit this life and do what he wanted to do, join General Jackson. Unless Lafitte meant he would continue to sail only as a supercargo now, keeping accounts.

Quartermaster Scovelli was awkwardly tracing a pencilled line on a chart. He laid it on the binnacle in front of Lee. "This your course. We go home. A hurricane is coming, Captain says. How he knows?" Scovelli gestured. "But he knows! Yes, always. So we signal the *Santa,* and though Captain You will beat his fists and swear—he too will go home. In three days, four days, we shall be anchored at Grand Terre, counting our money. No?"

He nudged Lee and strode to order signal flags.

CHAPTER FOURTEEN

THE BRITISH OFFER

The first ten days back at Grand Terre were busy ones. The organization of smugglers and pirates was operated, as might be expected of Jean Lafitte, like a large, well-run business in New Orleans. Strict account was kept of all goods taken from seized merchant vessels and of every Negro man, woman and child taken from captured slavers. There was a vast amount of bookkeeping and taking inventory after every voyage, and total figures of goods, slaves, and treasure had to be condensed on one sheet so that at any moment Lafitte could know the total wealth of the colony.

Every man received a share of the loot according to his rank, whether left on guard at Grand Terre or taken afloat as a seaman, navigator, officer, or captain. Periodically long lines formed around Warehouse 1 where the offices and strong-room were, and as each rough smuggler called out his name he was given his pay. Should he want goods instead of gold and silver, he could buy them at very low prices.

Furious celebrations followed each such division of treasure. Drinking, gaming, and carousing continued night and day for perhaps a week. Quarrels broke out, and men were shot and stabbed. But quarrels did not halt the flow of liquor, the clink of coins, or the boisterous singing. A celebration ended only when most smugglers were again penniless. Gradually then the colony pulled itself together; and the freebooters soon were again at sea.

Captured vessels were stripped of gear useful on the smugglers' ships. Sometimes cannon were mounted on their decks and they were added to the already impressive fleet. A busy shipyard was part of the Barataria Bay colony. Five large warehouses containing loot were another part. A well-guarded stockade enclosing shabby huts was the section where Negroes were kept until auctioned. Scattered here, there, everywhere over the verdant island were the shacks, shanties, and cabins of crewmen, some with wives and families, others living carelessly in twos or threes.

Lee found himself working under the direction of Doc, the trusted head bookkeeper. A bony little man, his head bald as an egg, Doc lacked a right leg below the knee and told Lee he had amputated it himself, indicating that once he must have been a surgeon. Now he was a wizard at figures, seeming to remember the location of every slave, every bolt of cloth, and every cask of rum on the island.

"Five bolts of white challis? With blue dots? In Warehouse 4," Doc would say amid asthmatic wheezes. "Two plantation boys about twenty?

We've got two brothers, nineteen and twenty-one. Four hundred dollars. A fine buy."

Doc supervised a staff of five who kept track of the loot. He reported frequently to Jean Lafitte, and with French Frank, the treasurer, supervised the twice-weekly auctions attended by many plantation owners and New Orleans and Natchez merchants.

Gradually Doc fell into the habit of sending Lee on errands to the cottage of Jean Lafitte on the little hill overlooking the Bay. Lee liked this, both because he could not help but admire the smuggler chief and because his home was quiet and pleasant and always in perfect order—in contrast with almost every other at Grand Terre. It was a cottage, richly furnished with fine carpets, gilded tapestry chairs and shining mahogany chests, and bright silken window draperies. There was even a beautiful piano shining with mother-of-pearl inlay. The mistress of the cottage was a small, dark Frenchwoman housekeeper, assisted by two or three Negro slaves.

Often Lee found Lafitte seated on his veranda or lying in a hammock staring across Barataria Bay. Sometimes he would be reading, sometimes conferring with his lieutenants or with gentlemen come to attend the auctions advertised regularly in the *Louisiana Gazette*. Once Lee had to wait until Mr. Livingston and another lawyer named Mr. Grymes departed, but he got no opportunity to speak to the man who had his money in safe-keeping.

Although Lafitte kept urging the lawyers on, they had been unable yet to free Pierre, still imprisoned for trial as a smuggler. This worried Jean, who feared an ill effect on Pierre's health. He himself had spent four years in a Spanish prison—so Lee heard—which explained why he was so bitter against Spain.

One day Lee waited for Lafitte to finish writing an order to Doc. Putting down his quill, the smuggler king eyed him in the steady, silent way he had. "I am told you refused your share of yesterday's division of money. Why?"

Lee shifted weight. "I don't need funds, sir."

"You are still opposed to our—business? And do not mean ever to accept your share of its reward?"

"Well—perhaps," Lee decided, "sometime I'll buy as many Negroes as I can and take them to some school to be trained and later set them free."

Jean Lafitte smiled. "As you like." He got several papers together and handed them to Lee.

"Sir," he ventured, "can you give me any news of our war with Britain?"

Lafitte strolled out on the wide veranda and sank into his hammock. "The news from the north is frankly bad. A British army has captured Washington and burned the capital, although they later withdrew. Philadelphia may be attacked next. Thanks to your General Jackson, our record is better in the south. He and a Major Lawrence kept the

British from seizing Fort Bowyer, near Mobile, several months ago. Then Jackson moved on to Pensacola and bottled up the British there with the Spaniards they suddenly love so well. Possibly General Jackson has already started west again. The government has finally recognized his ability by making him a major general in the regular army.

"I have reason to believe," he went on, "that the British Colonel Nicholls plans to seize the mouth of the Mississippi and that another force will take Baton Rouge. Thus he will cut off New Orleans by sea and land until he starves it into submission. He has circulated a proclamation in New Orleans urging the French and Spanish there to rise up against what he calls 'the American yoke.' Through his agents, he also encourages the slaves to revolt."

Lee reflected a moment. "When do you think the British will take the river mouth, sir?"

"At any moment. They have a formidable fleet at their disposal and may land as many as ten thousand troops for an attack on New Orleans. These men are veteran regulars; probably some of them fought under Wellington in the Peninsular campaign against Napoleon. Meanwhile," Lafitte continued acidly, "General Jackson has called upon Governor Claiborne and Commandante Patterson at New Orleans to improve the city's defenses and raise troops. But they, in their laziness, do nothing to prepare for the calamity which may engulf them."

He seemed to regard the interview as ended. Lee moved to the edge of the veranda to leave, then raised a hand to shade his eyes as he stared at the entrance of Barataria Bay to the Gulf. "Sail ho!"

Remembering he was not on shipboard, he turned. "Sir, is that not a strange vessel entering the bay? None of our fleet is expected!"

Jean Lafitte gave an exclamation and rose from his hammock. Swiftly he went into the cottage and returned at once with a long brass telescope. He kept it to his eye a long moment. Two cannon guarding the entrance to the bay boomed, and Lee knew two shots were hurtling across the bow of the vessel.

"Flies the Cross of St. George and a flag of truce," Lafitte murmured. "They're heaving to."

He lowered the telescope. "Order my small boat. Hurry!"

Lee ran down the path. When he reached the rotting wharf, Guinea George, bos'n of Lafitte's whaleboat, already was rounding up his six-man crew as if he guessed they would be wanted.

Lafitte came hurrying down the path. His wavy brown hair tossed in the wind. Looking now like the commonest of his seamen, he wore a plain green shirt open at the throat, a brace of pistols thrust inside a broad leather belt, and plain dark trousers.

"Man the whaleboat!" Guinea George sang out.

Lafitte beckoned to Lee. "Have you writing materials? I may need you." He dropped into the small boat, Lee following suit. Lafitte called to one of his captains watching ashore, the Italian named Ilo. "Assemble a boarding party and hold them ready. If I do not return in an hour, or if that brig raises sail to leave, rescue me!"

"Maybe ees trick. Let me go," Ilo urged.

Lafitte shook his head. Next moment the oarsmen pulled the whaleboat around, and bending to a rhythmic stroke, made for the British man-o'-war.

As they drew near there was an exchange of hails. "Brig *Sophie*, Captain Lockyer. Also Captain McWilliams of the Royal Colonial Marines. Desire to see Monsieur Lafitte!" an officer called.

Lafitte merely replied that he would come aboard. A rope ladder was dropped from the *Sophie*, now anchored. Lafitte stood up, and as the whaleboat maneuvered close, seized the ladder and jumped to its bottom rung.

"Lee, you follow. Guinea George, you come with two men. Remain on deck if I go below with the gentlemen. No talking, mind! And keep your hands off your weapons unless there's real need for them."

He climbed agilely up the side and vanished onto the deck of the brig. Lee followed, then the three crewmen. In a moment they stood watching their leader greeting two British officers. One, who would be Captain Lockyer, was tall and elderly, clad in his blue dress naval uniform with much gold trimming. The other, sunburned and hard-looking, was Cap-

Lafitte Made Ready to Board the Ship

tain McWilliams of the Marines.

"We seek conference with your leader, Monsieur Lafitte," the Marine officer explained.

"I am Lafitte, gentlemen. At your service."

Lee noted the officers' exchange of surprised looks. "Shall we go below, Monsieur Lafitte?" Captain Lockyer suggested. "I wish to extend the hospitality of His Majesty's vessel, after which we will explain our errand."

"Your pardon, gentlemen," Lafitte replied suavely. "It appears that you are calling upon me more than I am calling upon you. And as the dinner hour approaches, will you not be so kind as to partake of my humble hospitality ashore? My facilities are meager, yet if you will honor me I shall do all possible to ensure your comfort."

Again the two officers exchanged looks. To reassure them, Lafitte smilingly added: "Your vessel will remain safely at anchor and you, of course, will return to her at your pleasure."

Captain McWilliams spoke up. "We accept, Monsieur, with thanks. An opportunity to walk on land will not be amiss after several days at sea."

"From Pensacola?" Lafitte inquired casually.

"From Mobile," Captain Lockyer corrected.

"Ah? Then Mobile is become a base for His Majesty's operations?"

"Doubtless Colonel Nicholls has occupied it by now. We shall join you ashore very shortly."

Lafitte went to the rail and climbed down the rope ladder, and Lee and the smugglers followed. While the oarsmen pulled for shore Lee wondered whether the British actually had taken Mobile. If so, how had General Jackson fared?

"I may need you, so remain within call," Lafitte told him as they reached the wharf. "Guinea George, dismiss your men. The errand of His Majesty's officers is a peaceful one, and I want no disturbance. See that hospitality is extended to their sailors—and see to't," he emphasized, "that hospitality does not turn into quarrels!"

Lee followed him to the cottage, soon being sent on various errands by the cricket-like little French housekeeper as preparations were hurriedly made to entertain the visitors. The finest of wines were brought from Jean Lafitte's personal cellar, the finest French linens laid, and hurriedly Raphael, the best chef in the smuggler colony, was summoned.

When the officers arrived before sundown Captain Ilo escorted them to the cottage. There Lafitte entertained them and served drinks on the veranda until the light was gone. There was nothing for Lee to do but remain near-by, and while he pondered on why the British had come he dined in the kitchen on the most toothsome food he had ever tasted.

After dinner the gentlemen repaired to the drawing room and took comfortable chairs for their conference. Save for the Frenchwoman entering now and again to offer more wine and the best of cigars, they were left undisturbed.

At nine o'clock the three men stood awhile on the veranda. Then Captain Ilo, who had been waiting, escorted them back to their small boat. Lafitte stood watching the half-dozen torches light up his visitors' way; then he turned and re-entered the cottage. For an hour Lafitte sat as if lost in thought.

At last the housekeeper came into the kitchen and beckoned. "He wishes you."

Lee went into the perfectly appointed drawing room. Lafitte seemed not to notice his presence, staring at the fireplace with a far-off glint in his eyes while a half-smile played on his lips.

At last, sobering, he looked up. "I have many men whom I could trust to do an important errand. Yet I would have most confidence in you, if you will undertake this one. Mind, I do not give you an order. But I think it is something you will want to do, and therefore may do well."

"Yes, sir."

"This errand involves the safety of Louisiana." He rose and turned his back to the fireplace, facing Lee. "Would you undertake a mission which should aid the United States in its war with Britain?"

"Aye, sir! Gladly!"

Lafitte nodded. "Very well, then. In brief, His Majesty's officers desire me to join their side. They want my entire fleet to fight with theirs. The reward for our men would be amnesty from any and all charges of piracy. My own reward—" he smiled grimly "—would be freedom from prison for my brother Pierre. Also a captaincy in His Majesty's navy, a certain sum in gold, and assurance that Grand Terre would not be molested, nor our activities in the Caribbean, and protection from the raid being planned by the United States navy under command of Mr. Patterson."

Lee's eyes widened. "Raid now being planned, sir?" he echoed. "On Grand Terre?"

"Yes, against Grand Terre. For, as you know, Governor Claiborne thinks very ill of our efforts to provide his citizens with goods and slaves at low prices and without paying customs duties. Only recently the Governor offered five hundred dollars reward for my capture."

"He did!"

Jean Lafitte chuckled. "In return, I advertised in New Orleans papers my offer of thirty thousand dollars for the capture of the Governor. Of the two of us, don't you consider I was the most flattering?"

Lee could only stare at this strange and brilliant man.

"However," Lafitte shrugged, "my levity in offering a reward for His Excellency's capture may have angered him so that now injured vanity may overbalance his judgment. That is why I send you on this errand. You are not really one of us—er, pirates, as some call us. But you are—as I am—a loyal American. So you must plead your very best, because it is for our country's sake."

He stopped. "Can you do this well?"

"I'll try, sir! But—perhaps I don't fully understand. What am I to tell Governor Claiborne in addition to the British offer to you?"

"Everything is written here." He indicated a packet of papers. "I have informed the British that it will take me fifteen days to put my affairs in order. They think—though I did not actually promise—that I am going to accept their offer. So we have fifteen days, Governor Claiborne and I, to join forces against them.

"My men will take you by boat to New Orleans. You should reach it by morning. There you will consult with Monsieur Jean Blanque, a member of the legislature whose name is on this packet. With him you will confer with the Governor, showing him these papers. Do your errand and return with the Governor's reply as swiftly as possible, since time is precious. Do you understand?"

"Yes, sir."

"Start, then." He offered his hand, and Lee took it. "If you do this well, you are free to leave my service when you will. And your contribution to our war against Britain will have been much greater than you could make as a private soldier serving with General Jackson. Good luck!"

CHAPTER FIFTEEN

GENERAL JACKSON ARRIVES

Governor William C. Claiborne, a handsome, well-set-up man of fifty, paced up and down his luxuriously furnished office in the Executive Mansion. He had his hands clasped behind his back, his head lowered. His footsteps were alternately muffled by the thick Persian rugs and ringing hollowly as he crossed the spaces of polished floor.

Lee, seated tensely on the edge of a fragile gilt chair against one wall, watched in hopeful silence. In another chair Monsieur Jean Blanque, a dark, gaunt gentleman, sat molding his hands while he kept his bird-like eyes on the Governor.

More relaxed and wearing dogged looks, Master Commandante Patterson of the United States Navy and Colonel Ross, 44th United States Infantry, waited in other chairs. They watched as the Governor paused beside his desk, his eyes on Lee Baird.

"You swear that you accompanied Lafitte aboard this British vessel, the *Sophie*? And that what you have told us is true?"

"Yes, sir, it is exactly as I have told you. Although Monsieur Lafitte has evaded the customs laws," Lee added earnestly, "he considers himself an American.

He does not wish to fight with the British. Else why would he send me here asking for your permission to join his forces with yours?"

"It is all a fabrication," Commandante Patterson growled.

Governor Claiborne pursed his lips. "I must admit, gentlemen, there is in this city a much greater disaffection than I had anticipated. And among faithful Louisianians there is a despondency which palsies my preparations for defense. Lafitte and his associates might prove very useful to us."

"Not if we can't trust him, Governor."

Colonel Ross spoke. "I agree with Commandante Patterson. Lafitte cannot be trusted. He may somehow have learned that our raid on Grand Terre takes place tonight. This is his wily scheme for urging us to delay until he can evacuate the place."

Lee suppressed a start. So engrossed were these gentlemen that they seemed not to realize they were revealing an important secret to a Lafitte man. Then the raid was planned for tonight.

He must let Jean Lafitte know that! The instant he was dismissed with Governor Claiborne's reply he would hurry to Grand Terre and warn the smuggler king that the meager forces of the United States were to be used, not in preparing against the British, but to wreck Grand Terre!

"Sir," he pleaded to the Governor, "Monsieur Lafitte, in his way, is a sincere man. He is an honorable

Governor Claiborne Paced the Floor

man, well esteemed in New Orleans. Does not his sincerity shine through his letter?"

Claiborne studied him. "You are but a youth, just sprouting your first beard. Yet you claim friendship with Andrew Jackson and with this rascal Lafitte, and a great deal else. Your story is difficult to accept."

He picked up Lafitte's letter from his desk and studied it. Although each man in the room had read it, Governor Claiborne repeated parts aloud:

" 'This point of Louisiana that I occupy is of great importance in the present situation. I offer myself to defend it. I am the lost sheep that desires to return to the flock . . .'

"Then," Governor Claiborne went on, "he says: 'In case, Monsieur Le Gouverneur, that your reply should not be favorable to my ardent wishes, I declare to you that I leave immediately so not to be held to have co-operated with an invasion of our land. This cannot fail to take place, and puts me entirely at the judgment of my conscience.' "

"Conscience?" Colonel Ross derided. "Has a smuggler a conscience?"

Monsieur Blanque leaned forward. "We must accept this offer! Else we invite much worse disaster than mere smuggling. That can be dealt with at any time. The burning question now is, are our military forces sufficient to repel assault and capture of New Orleans by the British, who will bring five times our numbers?"

"What do you say, gentlemen?" Governor Claiborne asked.

"Battles are won," Colonel Ross said stiffly, "by strategy, not by numbers of men."

"Exactly," nodded the naval commander. "Besides, President Madison would not countenance trafficking with a lawbreaker for any reason."

There was silence. "Then you oppose acceptance of Lafitte's proposal?" Governor Claiborne asked.

"It is a pack of lies, a trick!"

"I definitely oppose acceptance. We should be ruined," growled Commandante Patterson.

Monsieur Blanque looked discouraged. Governor Claiborne tapped his fingers on the desk, pondering. "I confess I am inclined to accept Lafitte's help and prosecute his lawbreaking later. Yet I must heed the advice of my military advisers. I shall write a rejection to Lafitte, and this young man can take it to him. I thank you gentlemen and must not keep you longer." He glanced out a window. "We have already used up the day; it is near sundown."

Blanque opened his mouth to protest the decision, then gloomily changed his mind and stalked from the room. Patterson and Ross, their swords clanking, bowed to the Governor and also departed. Lee, at a gesture, remained where he was.

For several moments Governor Claiborne wrote his reply. Waiting, Lee was heavy-hearted and yet at the same time anxious to be off to Grand Terre. He would carry the bad news of the Governor's rejection of Lafitte's assistance—but also the vitally important news that the long-expected raid was to come this very night!

The Governor sealed the letter and handed it to Lee. "Just a moment," he said, reflecting. Then he turned and wrote another letter.

Sealing it, he looked at Lee. "Although I reject Lafitte's offer, I feel that General Jackson should know of it. He will assume command of our defense, and he should arrive tonight—"

"Tonight!" Lee exclaimed.

"Yes. Since you claim acquaintance with the General, I want you to take this second letter to him *before* you go to Grand Terre. Do you understand?"

Lee thought fast. "Sir, I am in the service of Monsieur Lafitte. Therefore, perhaps another courier could go to General Jackson—"

"Ah! Then you lied when you claimed acquaintance?"

Lee sprang to his feet. "No, sir! I do not lie! But you have others who could carry your—"

"They will not do. I want you to tell your story to General Jackson as you have told it to me." The Governor's eyes narrowed. "Perhaps I had best send you to him under guard. Then—"

"No, sir—'twill not be necessary. At your command I will gladly go to General Jackson," Lee interrupted hastily. He was fearful lest, in custody of some aide, he have no opportunity to warn Lafitte of Commandante Patterson's raid.

Governor Claiborne eyed him intently. "I can rely on you?"

"I give my word, sir."

"Very well. Here is the letter. When you have seen General Jackson you are free to go to Lafitte, but not before. You will find the General, I believe, somewhere near Lake Pontchartrain."

Lee turned to leave. As he neared the door it opened and one of the secretaries dashed in.

"Your Excellency, Pierre Lafitte has escaped!"

Lee stood staring. Governor Claiborne rose from his desk. "What! You are certain?"

"Word has just come from the Presbytere. For days rascally smugglers sent by his brother Jean must have been tunnelling under the building. Lafitte escaped not an hour ago!"

Lee swallowed hard. Recollecting himself, he quietly passed the secretary and made his way out of the executive mansion.

Forty minutes later he was sauntering casually into a tavern only a half-block from the very point of the levee where the auction of the *Cumberland Belle's* cargo from Tennessee had been held months before. He paused in the tavern doorway to glance up and down the dark street lighted here and there by a yellow whale oil lamp.

Inside, he went straight to the bulky, hairy man who sat drinking with his back turned. As Lee dropped into another chair at his table Captain Dominique You's eyes gleamed impatiently.

"Monsieur Le Gouveneur requires all day to decide his mind?"

"We sat there for hours. He refuses."

Dominique You started. Anger flushed his dark countenance and he banged his fist on the little table. "Refuses? *Mon dieu!* How can he do thees? I, who was once a foremost artillerist of the army of France, can plainly see New Orleans has but a feeble defense! Does not Le Gouverneur realize? Thees British, they may enter at will! He ees a fool! Why will he not use the men and sheeps and weapons of Grand Terre? Thees cannot be!"

Lee nodded. "It's true. But listen, Captain." He glanced around to make certain they were not overheard. "I have to carry an important dispatch to General Jackson. He is somewhere on the edge of the city. Maybe I can convince him to use Monsieur Lafitte's help though I failed to convince the Governor. It would be just as good, perhaps better, wouldn't it?"

Captain You stared at him. He examined a corner of the tavern ceiling. He looked again at Lee. "*Mais oui.* The General will have command, not Le Gouverneur. No? Therefore ees important you convince him how we assist. Yes! you do not, then, return to

Grand Terre with me. I explain why not you come—"

"You must hurry back, Captain, starting at once. By the way," Lee said with pretended casualness, "did you know that Pierre Lafitte had escaped?"

The wily You did not react quickly enough. "Ees true? What you t'ink!"

Lee smiled grimly. "You knew, Captain—I can tell! But listen." Hurriedly he explained about the raid planned for tonight by the few vessels of the United States navy. Captain You cocked his head. He rose with fists doubled.

"At once I go. Through the canals and swamps I am faster than those barnacle-bottom sheeps. Adieu!" He strode to the door but halted there; then chuckling a little he came back.

"Observe, Lee Baird. Ees not now good that I once, a year ago, give you the drugged wine to drink? So you have learn all this of importance? You forgive that I do eet, eh?"

Lee considered. A little grudgingly he nodded.

You clapped his shoulder. "Good! I was but playeeng. Did you theenk I would harm you? No! Now I go!" And he hurried out.

Having eaten nothing since before noon, Lee hurried to the café a few doors down the street. He was weary despite several hours sleep gained while Captain You and two other smugglers brought him overnight by small boat the sixty miles to New Orleans. But the food gave him a feeling of freshness and when he gained the street again he was eager to locate General Jackson.

His first act was to hire a horse. Then, inquiring his way of an occasional soldier found in the streets, he headed for Fort St. Jean on Lake Pontchartrain, located northeast of the city. In the dark he had to trust to his roan's keen alertness for good footing, but kept the horse at a trot as much as possible. It was a little before midnight when he approached dying campfires that marked the army encampment.

A sentry hailed Lee and he reined in. The man called another guard and the pair advanced cautiously. "Who are you?"

"Lee Baird. I knew General Jackson in Nashville. I bear important dispatches from Governor Claiborne and I must see the General personally!"

"Humph! Stay where you are." The two sentries withdrew a few paces to confer. One returned and ordered Lee to dismount. The other presently reappeared with the officer of the guard.

Lee repeated his story. "Sir, my dispatches have to do with the safety of New Orleans. I must hurry!"

"Very well. Orson, escort this man to headquarters."

Lee led his horse, the soldier walking beside him. He inquired what campaigns the man had been in and learned he had been enlisted at Nashville.

"Ain't so many of us originals left," the soldier

declared. "We had dysentery and typhoid and Injuns and British and just about everything. Lots o' the boys died. Some quit and went home. Ain't had our pay regular for months. Ain't had decent grub—and ain't got any now. Those blasted army contractors!" he growled. "Flour full o' weevils, bacon a-moldin'—"

He broke off as two guards before a small farmhouse challenged them. There was more parley but at last Lee was ushered indoors to a room smoky from many candles, where a narrow-faced man in faded uniform sat with half a dozen officers grouped close around him, pouring over maps.

The aide accompanying Lee clicked his heels and saluted. "Sir, dispatches from Governor Claiborne."

Without looking up General Jackson thrust out his hand. Lee took the sealed letter from inside his shirt and placed it in the hand. It was bony and shook as from palsy. Then he saw General Jackson's face, and his heartbeat slowed in dismay.

For Jackson, a victim of acute dysentery, had lost much of his always sparse flesh. His face had a greenish pallor, like that of a man utterly sick but dragging himself about by sheer will power. If he had looked unwell when Lee saw him some months ago at The Hermitage, he looked almost dying now.

The piercing gray eyes rose to Lee. Thrusting back his chair, Jackson came around the table. "And how is your filly these days, lad? Can she still run?"

He was amazed at the instant recognition, for he had grown taller and heavier and was deeply tanned. "Faith, she can run, sir. But she's a three-year-old mare now, and perhaps old enough to race Truxton!"

General Jackson and his officers laughed heartily. The General pumped his hand and clapped him on the shoulder. "Aye, and perhaps she'll get her chance! But you look well, Lee, indeed."

"And you, sir—" He hesitated. "Are you quite well?"

"From those Benton wounds? Yes, long ago. From other causes—no," Jackson said, and suddenly looked very tired, "I am not well. Yet sickness must be postponed. There is important work. Tell me, what are you doing here?"

"Your pardon, General. First I wish to say that the proceeds from sale of your goods on the keelboat are safe. Nearly six thousand dollars. Mr. Livingston, a respected lawyer of New Orleans, is keeping it for you together with my own funds."

Jackson cocked his head. "Gentlemen, Lee Baird of Nashville," he introduced him to his officers. "Lee is the son of Sergeant Adam Baird whom some of you knew in years past." He turned back. "I had all but forgotten personal matters, I've been so out of touch. But you say I own near six thousand dollars? And 'tis with Edward Livingston? Ah, that's welcome news. I'd thought I must be penniless!"

Jackson Recognized Lee Instantly

He asked a few questions as to what Lee had been doing, and his sharp eyes showed surprise when he related his association with Jean Lafitte. "That rascal!" Remembering Governor Claiborne's letter, he broke its seal and read it quickly.

"Hm. This is strange." He outlined its contents to his officers. "Sit down, Lee. What have you to say about this British offer to buy Lafitte's services?"

For two hours Lee was keep busy answering questions and reiterating the sincerity of Jean Lafitte's desire to side with American forces in the defense of New Orleans. He told of Commandante Patterson's raid which must be in progress at this moment, explaining frankly that he had warned Captain You, who would in turn have warned the men at Grand Terre. His entire story was given with readiness, including his account of the day-long conference in Governor Claiborne's office; he saw that he had made an impression.

"Let us sum up," Jackson said at last. "I trusted you with my goods, Lee, and I trust you now for accurate information. You believe that Jean Lafitte sincerely means to help us against the British if we'll accept his help?"

"I do, sir. Provided there is much of his fleet left after tonight," he remembered.

"What is his strength?" an officer asked.

"Forty-seven vessels of various sizes a week ago today. Some, of course, are at sea. And just over a thousand men, all experienced fighters."

There was silence. General Jackson leaned back in his chair. "I am reluctant to be aided by this lawbreaker and his hellish banditti."

Two or three of his officers exchanged looks. "But General," one protested, "we shall be hard pressed to defend New Orleans with its six main approaches. We must guard all, not knowing where the Redcoats will strike."

"Our troops will be outnumbered and the British better trained and equipped," another reminded.

"And with their fleet, they doubtless will have far superior artillery, General."

"We are missing General Coffee's force, also the two thousand men which the War Department indicated are on the way from Tennessee."

"We'll have to rely heavily on local volunteers," another urged. "Many of these New Orleans dandies have never smelled gunpowder. Even their loyalty is uncertain, since they are of French and Spanish descent."

General Jackson listened, frowning. "True, gentlemen. Our task looks now to be impossible. Yet I dislike to join forces with a smuggler.

"Lee," he said, "go with Lieutenant York, who will provide you lodging. We cannot settle this tonight. You are tired, and I have work to do—much work, since I take command of New Orleans at seven in the morning."

CHAPTER SIXTEEN

THE ASSAULT BEGINS

It was December 1, 1814 when Andrew Jackson and his twenty-five hundred weary and ill-equipped troops occupied New Orleans. The battle which ensued for its defense was not a single furious engagement ending in a decision, but a series of clashes over more than a month before the final bloody fight at Rodriguez Canal.

During the first week of December, Lee was kept busy as a courier between Jean Lafitte and gentlemen of New Orleans who still hoped he and his forces would be accepted by General Jackson. Lee's first task after resting that night at Fort St. Jean was to locate Lafitte and learn about the raid of Commandante Patterson's flotilla carrying troops under Colonel Ross. He set about the very next morning contacting Lafitte agents who always were scattered throughout the city.

But the raid had frightened them into hiding and it was a two-day search before he found the first of the smuggler band. This was Scovelli, who had been quartermaster on the *Cartagena.* Lee found Scovelli moodily tipsy in a little tavern on Royal Street, a bandage around his head and one arm in a sling.

"What a fight! More bad than with a French frigate," Scovelli sighed. "But most escaped before those ruffians arrived. Only I was peacefully slipping—"

"Slipping?" Lee said, puzzled.

"But yes, slipping!" Scovelli put his head on his hands and snored to indicate sleeping. "Under a table peacefully I was slipping. So my comrades, they leave without me. So I fight those soldier almost single with my hands!"

Pierre Lafitte, Lee learned, had joined his brother at Grand Terre only an hour or so before the attack. That it was coming had just been learned from Captain Dominique You. For the most part, Grand Terre was abandoned when the United States navy and army forces struck. The hundreds of smugglers, some with wives and children, had swiftly put to sea leaving everything behind. They were scattered now from Grand Terre up the Mississippi to places above New Orleans, and all the way along the Gulf coast to Galvez Town.

Grand Terre had been rifled and burned. Goods worth half a million dollars had been brought to New Orleans, and although the raid had been almost bloodless, Commandante Patterson claimed a great victory.

The Lafittes were safe in a small camp at Cote Allemand, a stretch of river above New Orleans. On learning this, Lee made his way there and reported what had happened during his call on Governor Claiborne and also the reception General Jackson had given him.

Pierre and Jean Lafitte listened in silence. Pierre was restlessly pacing the floor of the plantation house they occupied, but Jean was as usual calm and deliberate. "The General is being obstinate," he murmured. "I'll write a letter which I want you to take to Mr. Livingston. He has been our counsel and it may be he can talk to the General."

So Lee returned to New Orleans and presented himself to Mr. Livingston. The lawyer recalled his face at once, though not his name. When Lee showed the receipt he had kept for a year for the seven thousand dollars in gold, Mr. Livingston's handsome countenance broke into smiles.

"Yes, now I know you! I wondered if you would ever return, young man—or whether I could keep the money for myself."

Lee grinned. "I thank you for keeping it, sir. I hope you will not object to keeping it longer, since I have no use for it now. I have told General Jackson that he may call on you for his portion. But I come, sir, from Monsieur Lafitte with this letter."

Livingston read it, then thought a moment. "I shall call on the General in this matter. Will you return for whatever news I gain—say tomorrow?"

The news was bad. General Jackson did not wish the assistance of Lafitte or any of his band.

There were other means, however, of bringing the advantage of using the Lafittes to General Jackson's attention. At the insistence of Mr. Livingston, several committees of citizens called on Jackson. Lee was summoned to military headquarters at 106 Royal Street late the first week and there questioned for two hours by Jackson's officers concerning the smugglers. Then he was admitted to the General's presence. The information he had given was retold. At last Jackson nodded.

"If you can, bring him here tomorrow evening. Colonel," he said to an aide, "kindly make out a safe-conduct for this Lafitte."

It was late the following evening when Lee and the ordinary-looking man with him were admitted to the headquarters building. No one questioned their safe-conduct and they were led to an office and left there several minutes alone. Lafitte, composed as always, sat as if resting, though Lee wanted to pace the floor with the uneasiness he felt.

A door opened and General Jackson entered. Lee got to his feet. "Good evening, sir. General Jackson—Monsieur Jean Lafitte."

Jackson bowed and the smuggler, with a quiet smile, bowed in return. The General waved Lafitte to a chair and took one himself. He offered cigars which Lafitte and Lee declined. Jackson busied himself lighting one. "I have said harsh things about you, Mr. Lafitte. Some have appeared in print."

"They were rather inaccurate, General," the smuggler smiled.

"I trust that is so. Certainly you have many friends in New Orleans who regard you highly. And certainly," he continued, "I find myself pledged to defend this city with insufficient men and arms. It is a time when all Americans must rally to our cause. As you well know, British capture of New Orleans means control of the Mississippi valley as well as of the Gulf coast. To lose New Orleans is unthinkable. It could well cost the United States the war."

"I know. You spoke of Americans rallying together, General," Lafitte reminded in his quiet voice.

Jackson studied him keenly. "We need not bandy words, sir. You regard yourself as American?"

"Yes."

"And your men?"

"They will follow me. We are somewhat disorganized, but that is a temporary condition."

"I do not offer a share of command, Mr. Lafitte. I offer an opportunity to serve under my command or such command as I designate."

"I understand, General. I ask for nothing except the opportunity to fight the British."

"You could have summoned the British a few nights ago to help you resist the raid on Grand Terre. They were within reach with their fleet. That, sir, is what tipped the scales of my judgment very definitely in your favor. It is the final proof I

"My Forces Are at Your Command, Sir."

sought that—well," Jackson said frankly, "that you are sincere in offering to battle the Redcoats."

"They are enemies of my country. Although I may have violated a few of our laws," Lafitte shrugged, "I have allegiance in my heart. I ask no terms, no special consideration. My forces are at your command."

General Jackson rose. To Lee's surprise he was smiling and offering Lafitte his hand. "We are, then, comrades in arms. My staff officers will suggest duties and placement of your forces if you will confer with them tomorrow at ten in this building. For the most part, I think we shall use your forces between Barataria and New Orleans."

"I have some expert artillerists and various cannon ranging from twelve to twenty-four pounders which can be used ashore."

"Excellent!"

"One thing, General," Lafitte added politely. "If the Federal government's pursuit of myself and my brother and our men could be postponed until after hostilities—" He did not finish but his meaning was clear.

"Else you will be jailed and unable to fight? Quite true. I shall ask the Federal court in the morning to postpone prosecution. I think this will be done.

"Well, Lee," he said, turning, "you have done good work. I confess we greatly need Mr. Lafitte in our defense. You scarcely thought back in Nashville that we should be in conference like this, eh?"

For several days Lee accompanied Lafitte while he conferred with the staff officers of Jackson's army. Although he did not sit in at all conferences, he gradually learned the great difficulties confronting any plan of defense of New Orleans.

There were six routes by which the enemy, with his great number of vessels and troops, could approach. The main route was the wide, muddy Mississippi; but this way was well guarded by Fort Philip below the city. West of the river wound the Bayou LaFourche, a narrow, deep stream which was in reality a branch of the Mississippi. Another route on the west was Barataria Bay, seventy miles from the two mouths of the mighty river. From Barataria a series of canals, bayous, and swamps made a tortuous water highway which the Lafittes had used between Grand Terre and New Orleans. To patrol these little-known and never-mapped waterways was the duty assigned to the few vessels which Jean Lafitte rounded up after the raid.

East of the river lay two sluggish streams, River aux Chenes, and Bayou Terre aux Boeufs. Both were navigable by small craft as far as English Turn, fourteen miles below the city. Another avenue of approach was Lake Borgne, an arm of the Gulf reaching close to the Mississippi just above English Turn. Possession of Lake Borgne would give the enemy two comparatively easy marching routes into

New Orleans—one, a narrow belt of flat land a mile wide, and the other five miles of reedy land interlaced with small bayous.

It had been General Jackson's expectation for many months that the British, when they were ready for New Orleans, would land west of Mobile and march overland. Now he saw that such was not their plan. But what was? Apparently, the British fleet was going to try to utilize some of the waterways to come as close as possible to the city, so that the remaining marching distance would be short. The fleet thus could use their heavy cannon to protect the troops while landing.

But which of the six approaches would Admiral Sir Alexander Cochrane and General Sir Edward Pakenham, the British commanders, choose? That was the problem worrying Jackson and his staff, whose total forces of a few thousand must be ready for attack anywhere along many miles of front.

All odds were with the British, known to be superior in numbers and equipment. General Pakenham's troops were veterans, some having taken part months earlier in the seizure and burning of Washington. Others had fought in some of the campaigns against Napoleon. Admiral Cochrane's cannon-bristling vessels numbered fifty-odd sail of all rigs and sizes. The flagship was the *Tonnant*, now anchored amid the fleet off Ship and Cat islands.

So confident were the British that many officers

were accompanied by their wives, who expected to become residents of New Orleans after its capture. Officials were present who would take charge of the customs, the courts, and city offices. There was even a skeleton police force ready to operate once New Orleans had been won. And so confident had the British become that their first plan—which Jackson had guessed—to capture Fort Bowyer at Mobile, then march overland to New Orleans, had been abandoned as much too laborious. It would be simpler, Admiral Cochrane decided, to move close by vessel, then debark General Pakenham's army for the capture of the city.

Feverish efforts were being made by General Jackson, his staff, and volunteer citizens to organize as many troops as possible to resist the enemy. Several companies were already in existence in New Orleans, but their activities until now had been more social than military. Early in his command Jackson called a dress parade of all available troops and reviewed them in the Place D' Armes with Edward Livingston, whom he had made a colonel.

Lee, perched in a window of the Cabildo, saw the parade pass. The five main companies were the Carabiniers d'Orleans, the Foot Dragoons, the Francs, the Chasseurs, and the Louisiana Blues. All were gorgeously uniformed and marched proudly as if eager to prove their mettle under fire.

For a week Lee shuttled between Lafitte, constantly on the move organizing and placing his smugglers, and General Jackson's headquarters. Jackson too was forever moving, overseeing the placement of his forces as he sought to discover by British movements where the first blow would be struck.

It came unexpectedly on December eighth. The thunder of distant cannon reached New Orleans and the city fell in a hush of tense waiting. Then word came: a swarm of British vessels had overwhelmed and sunk five small United States gunboats under command of Lieutenant Thomas Catesby Jones. Lake Borgne, only a dozen miles away, was in enemy hands!

Panic swept through New Orleans. Many families packed their most precious belongings and fled northward. But most remained, even though they knew that British vessels must be standing close to shore on the Lake and rapidly discharging veteran troops.

The gunboats had been, as General Jackson said, his "eyes and ears on Lake Borgne." Now it was difficult to learn particulars of the enemy's movements. Did he mean to strike north from the Lake? Or would he seek only a skirmish there, a feint, while he struck in much greater strength elsewhere?

Jackson, though he had lost the first round of the fight, had no choice but to wait. He dared not assemble his strength against the Lake Borgne invasion until he knew it was to be the main scene of battle.

Nor, though many citizens were frightened, did Jackson seem to be. For thirty-six hours his Royal Street headquarters buzzed with activity and for thirty-six hours he did not sleep. New placements were made, new companies drilled by the hour in the streets. Dispatches were sent by swift horse to urge General Coffee somewhere north near Baton Rouge to hurry. General Billy Carroll had left Tennessee two months before and was expected but had not been heard from. Jackson hoped he would bring two thousand militiamen.

The city was under martial law. No vessels came or left. No one could be on the streets without a military pass.

The longed-for reinforcements finally arrived. On December 20 General Coffee's advance guard of eight hundred exhausted men reached a point four miles north of New Orleans. They had marched 135 miles in three days. Presently General Carroll's flatboats arrived, having been delayed by storms and high water. Wasting no time, Carroll had drilled his recruits aboard the flatboats during the journey, and now they were ready to fight.

On December 23 Lee waited at headquarters with a dispatch from Jean Lafitte for the General. There was a commotion outside; then a hatless young officer, his uniform muddy, his face pale, came dashing in from the street. Without hesitation he burst into Jackson's private office.

"Important! Highly important, General!" Lee heard him cry. "Our plantation—the Villere plantation—has been captured!"

Jackson gave an exclamation. "You are—?"

"Major Gabriel Villere, sir. The plantation is five miles above English Turn. The British overcame our patrols and sentries. I was on the veranda with my father after breakfast when suddenly the house was surrounded and we were taken. I managed to escape and came here at once," the young major panted.

There followed sharp questioning for details. General Jackson seemed to have a clear picture in his mind of the miles and miles around the city his troops were scattered, and what this British move meant.

"They've strengthened themselves above the Lake," he reflected. "For days they've had comparative freedom from interference, for we suspected they were but feinting. But by the eternal, they shall not sleep on our soil!" he cried.

His staff officers came running at his urgent summons. Lee listened, fascinated, as orders were barked, men rushed out, others came running in. Then to his astonishment the hubbub dwindled and he heard General Jackson calmly call for wine and glasses for his staff.

The wine was poured. Lee knew all were raising their glasses. "Gentlemen," General Jackson said, "the British are below. We must fight them tonight!"

Half an hour later he was able to deliver his dispatch. Jackson read it, dictated an immediate reply, and directed Lee to hasten back to Lafitte, some thirty miles toward Barataria. But his route, Lee knew, was away from where the fighting would take place, and perhaps his reluctance showed on his face as he started out of the room.

"Come back here!"

Lee re-entered the office and saluted. General Jackson's keen gray eyes held a faint twinkle despite their sternness.

"You young ex-farmer, riverman, and smuggler—don't you relish your duty?"

"Yes, sir. Although—" He hesitated. "Won't I see any fighting, sir?"

Jackson abruptly laughed and whacked his knee. "No, not today. But in a few days there'll be the real fighting. You want to be in that, do you?"

Impulsively Lee took a step forward. "Yes! I mustn't miss it! I've long wanted to join you, sir—for months and months—but something always interfered. Now I want to fight!"

Jackson glanced around at his officers. All were smiling broadly. "Very well. You shall fight, you young rooster. Not today, but when the real battle comes. Now be off!"

CHAPTER SEVENTEEN

TRUXTON AND VENUS

Capture of the Villere plantation just before Christmas had revealed a heavy concentration of British troops around Bayou Bienvenu, though the Americans had supposed the British regulars still aboard their fleet off Ship and Cat islands.

The battle was furious that cold misty night of December 24. For awhile the Americans gave ground under the weight of lead hurled at them by the well-drilled Redcoats. Retreating, the Americans left precious six-pound cannon exposed to capture.

Jackson dashed into the thick of the fighting. "Save the guns!" he shouted.

The soldiers rallied. A company of the 7th Infantry rushed to the rescue and the guns were saved.

"Charge! Give 'em the bayonet! *A la bayonette!*" Fighting along the Rodriguez Canal, General Coffee took several prisoners, one a Major Mitchell who had applied the torch to the Capitol in Washington. From the captives Jackson learned the distribution of British troops and knew that here, along the Canal and around the Villere plantation, the important battle would be fought.

An American soldier captured by the British told General Pakenham that Jackson's forces numbered twelve thousand. The American evidently believed this greatly exaggerated figure and so convinced his questioners. The unexpected number of Americans made the British delay their final assault, so that despite a minor clash from time to time the decisive battle was not fought until January 8, 1815.

Lee was in at the end, as Jackson had promised he would be. Assigned to the Baratarians' battery, Captain Dominique You commanding, he had learned that Lafitte's lieutenant was indeed an experienced artillerist. The battery was Number 3 in a row of eight along the Rodriguez Canal which ran in a northeasterly direction from the Mississippi. Captain You had drilled his men by the hour, and learning in the brief fighting on December 28 where his crews were inexpert, promptly drilled them harder than before.

It was cold and clammy camping on the ground beside the menacing twelve-pounders. For a week Lee had been stiff and cold at night, though it was better during the day while the sun shone. When the final battle would start, no one knew, but the men thought it significant one morning when General Jackson and several aides came past on inspection while heavy mist still shrouded the dawn.

They were clustered around the fire, dripping their coffee the Creole way. Suddenly the lean, sick-looking Jackson sat his horse close by. "That smells like better coffee than we get." He turned to Dominique You. "Did you smuggle it?"

"Mebbe so, General," You shrugged, and filling a cup, handed it to Jackson.

The General saw Lee and urged his horse forward a step. "Do you wish you were back in Nashville now, reading law?"

"There's time for that later, sir," Lee replied. "We've business here first."

Jackson laughed and moved on. There was half an hour of waiting. It was an uneasy time, for there was a feeling in the air of desperate events about to take place. The American forces were strung along the canal, infantry and artillery. They faced a field of high grass with a shallow ditch across it, then more grass, then another ditch. Far in the British rear were batteries hidden in a cane stubble in front of the shell-torn ruins of Chalmette plantation house. The enemy would come marching across that field and those ditches.

The slight breeze strengthened and the mist began to vanish. Then with a faint hissing a rocket speared into the gray sky far behind the British lines. In a moment another rocket answered from an enemy force deployed along the Mississippi. It seemed instantly that British batteries opened with thunderous roars.

"They want it now," Dominique You shrugged.

"We load!"

The men sprang to obey. Lee passed a heavy ball to the loader, who thrust it down the cannon's throat after a sack of powder. The matchman applied his fire. Another gun yards away pounded, then the one Lee served; and next moment the eight batteries roared in a hellish syncopation that made the earth quiver.

The mist was fading fast. "There they come!" a man cried.

For a moment Lee was too busy to look. In a lull while more shot were being rushed from the rear, he straightened. The high grass was clear for a matter of some two hundred yards. Beyond that moved thick masses of redcoated soldiers, their bayonets glinting menacingly in the sun.

The sight whisked his breath away. He watched in fascination as the two columns marched steadily forward. One was wading the two ditches at their north ends where they were shallowest. The other was rounding the north ends. Company after company of grim, veteran, well-drilled soldiers, the finest of His Majesty's arms!

"We keel those British battery," Dominique You grumbled. "Then we cut holes in those soldiers—no? Faster!" he ordered.

The guns throbbed, their recoil hurling them back two or three yards despite the mud and plank backing. At each firing they had to be shouldered forward into position, swabbed, and reloaded. The work went on steadily, grimly, and almost without words. If it had been cold before, Lee found himself drenched with perspiration now from his unceasing labor and suppressed excitement.

A shell landed in Number 2 battery. There was a tremendous explosion. When the debris showered down, the battery had disappeared.

"Come! Faster!" shouted Dominique You. "Maybe ees for us next. Before then we must show them!"

It seemed an hour that the din steadily increased and the battle heightened in fury. Near-by companies of infantry trotted past to take up breastwork positions. The heavy pound of cannon on both sides, the constant rattle of musketry seeming to steal slowly nearer, and the occasional screams of wounded made this seem another, stranger world—and a desperate one.

"They're breaking through!" came a cry on the left.

"We turn thees guns. Come—dig!" Dominique You gripped Lee's shoulder and pushed him to the first of the twelve-pounders. "Those shovels! Those mauls! Faster, you men!" he roared.

The smuggler's plan was swiftly apparent. The American battery at the end of the line had been silenced. Battery 6 had but one gun still working. Battery 5 had lost two. And those lines of enemy soldiers out in the grass still re-formed in the face

The Battle Heightened in Fury

of terrible musket fire—re-formed and came stolidly on as if defying death.

General Jackson rode past, his horse prancing with fright. "Turn your guns! Rake those Redcoats to the north!"

It was what Dominique You had already seen to be necessary. While his crewmen strained and grunted to change gun positions, the British rear batteries kept flinging over shells. Now, suddenly, they seemed to be landing closer. One tore a crater but a few feet from the Number 1 gun. Two men threw up their hands and pitched forward, dead. A spray of metal fragments rattled on the cannon Lee served.

Though the battle was on too large a scale for any one person to see it all, he could tell from the couriers racing past and the hoarse commands of officers that British manpower was crushing the north end of the American line. Reserve infantrymen trotted past with rifles alert. Batteries 8 and 7 now were blown to bits and smoking. Number 6 operated but two guns. Number 5 still fired occasionally, although several of its men had been killed by a shell. Number 4 lost an eighteen-pounder when it exploded.

The greater danger was as General Jackson had feared: he had been forced to spread his five thousand troops so thinly that a strong attack in one place might break through. And here, along the Rodriguez Canal, the British were driving fiercely in the face of terrible and constant fire.

The cannon plowed great gaps in the ranks of on-coming scarlet uniforms. American rifle fire accurately picked off officers and men in the advancing front ranks. But as they threw up their arms and pitched headlong, those in the next rank stepped over them, coming steadily on.

"Now!" yelled Dominique You when the first twelve-pounder had been turned at the new angle. "Load! Fire, queeck! Grape only we use—thees Redcoats!"

Even as he shouted, Lee glimpsed a scarlet uniform. A cold stab of dismay went through him at the realization that the British were so close. There was an officer waving his sword, calling on his men to storm the battery—

The twelve-pounder jumped with its explosion. Like men in a mirage, the British vanished. Yet when the smoke slowly lifted Lee saw a new swarm of those scarlet uniforms, glimpsed flashing bayonets, and knew that direct assault on his battery was here.

"Cutlasses! We board!"

Dominique You, in his excitement, used the term he had employed at sea to order the attacks on the crews of resisting frigates. But his men scarcely had needed the order. Their cannon too slow-firing, too cumbersome at close quarters, they turned to their small-arms piled handily behind the guns.

Lee snatched a pistol and a cutlass, and was straightening and turning when something sharp and hot streaked across his back. Vaguely he knew it had been a rifle ball. But he seemed to be all right. Then another bullet tore away his low-pulled cap and seemed to plow through his hair with a jerk that snapped his head back.

Scarcely noting it, he saw enemies closing in. Scovelli, quartermaster on the *Cartagena,* met a lanky Redcoat's saber slash with a parry, then whipped his weapon at the man's neck. But his blow died in the air, and reeling back, Scovelli went down with a sort of coughing sigh, a bullet in his chest.

It was a melee now—scarlet uniforms intermingled with the varied rough dress of the smugglers from Grand Terre. More and still more scarlet uniforms flooded into the battery. A soldier leveling his rifle at Lee was shot between the eyes and fell like a clubbed ox, his gun discharging wildly.

Lee's pistol bullet took another Redcoat in the shoulder. Still another rushed around the cannon's length. He aimed his pistol but it did not explode. Then he and Lee struck together, clubbing their pistols, stabbing with sword and cutlass at too close quarters to be effective.

Men jostled their elbows. Punching, gouging, kicking, clubbing with their weapons, the mixture of British and Americans were a squirming mass. Lee, stepping backward, went into a hole of the cannon's former position. Staggering, he dodged a vicious sweep of sword; then recovering his balance, he plunged at his adversary. His cutlass-point slashed the officer's coat as the man whipped sideways; but it took him high in the chest and involuntarily he gulped a cry of pain. He went down, and before Lee could seek another foe, two husky grenadiers came at him.

In sudden panic he realized that the Baratarians were dead, wounded, or scattering. One short, burly member of his gun crew was close by Lee's shoulder . . . Dominique You! They were a tiny island in a sea of scarlet.

"A la bayonette!"

The shrill cry came from somewhere behind. Though he heard it, Lee was too fiercely busy slashing, jabbing, thrusting with his bloody-bladed cutlass to give heed. But next moment the mass of scarlet uniforms before and around him seemed to reel back. The burly Captain You beside him clubbed his pistol savagely at an enemy's face, jabbed another with his cutlass, bumped into Lee.

It was wild and disorganized fighting, with every man for himself. Dimly he knew reserves had been thrown into the line at this point. The small-arms din heightened; the scarlet uniforms seemed to be thinning. He himself had killed or badly wounded that brindle-bearded grenadier, that stubby Redcoat—he could not tell how many. But he was swinging and slashing his cutlass as he recovered inch by inch the ground he had yielded.

There came a sharp cry close beside him. Glancing, Lee saw Dominique You reel at a sword-thrust into his side. The officer who had adroitly penetrated the smuggler's defense drew his sword back and slashed with it again straight at You's chest.

Lee, with a frantic effort, threw himself against the officer's left side. The force of his blow knocked the man staggering. It saved Dominique You's life, but the next instant a rifle bullet plowed a groove across his temple.

Vivid red, purple, and green sparks sprayed in his brain. His muscles went abruptly watery. He seemed to be spilling headlong over a high cliff . . .

That was all he knew.

It was all he knew until, long afterward, he felt himself being carried by two men. Limply Lee peered about with paining eyes. He was puzzled that it was night and he no longer seemed to be on the battlefield. Then he was put down into something soft. It was, he decided, a cot. He seemed to be in a large hall—or no, this was a church. He could hear groans around him of others wounded, low talk, and footsteps of persons passing. He saw Creole gentlewomen of New Orleans move silently about nursing American and British alike after the invaders had been thoroughly routed and hurled back in confusion from the city's very gates.

It was several days later that Dominique You and Jean Lafitte entered the church to visit their wounded comrades of Grand Terre. Lee, feeling better save for the constant headache caused by his wound, saw them coming, caught the quick, dark eyes of the stocky smuggler.

"Ah! Here ees he who save my life! Come." Captain You beckoned to Lafitte, just ending a talk with another of his former crew. The hairy captain hurried to Lee's side. Despite his arm in a sling, a thick bandage over his chest, and another covering one eye, he seemed to have his usual vigor. "How ees, eh? You maybe die?"

"No. Some other time, perhaps. Good day, sir," he greeted Lafitte.

"I am glad to see you, Lee. You will recover?"

"Yes, sir. It wasn't too bad a wound. In a few weeks, I hope, I'll be leaving for—" He paused.

"Tennessee?"

"Yes, sir. And you gentlemen?" he queried.

They exchanged smiles. "General Jackson seemed pleased with the aid our men gave in the battle. He is petitioning President Madison in Washington for a full pardon for all of us. So we shall be good citizens again," Lafitte said, his eyes twinkling, though he spoke in his usual quiet tone.

Lee nodded as much as his head bandage would permit. "I'm glad, sir. And the war? How is it going?"

Captain You's brows went up. "What! Have not zey told? Ees ended! Thees British, they go back to their sheeps—pft! Gladly they sail. Now are all gone. And whole war ees over. In truth, was peace signed by United States and England many days before thees battle here!"

It took Lee a moment to digest this information. "You mean the war was really over before our battle?"

"Yes," Lafitte nodded. "The news reached us only yesterday that peace has been declared. Still, it was a great victory for General Jackson. Else perhaps they would have tried to keep New Orleans and the whole Gulf coast."

"And General Jackson?"

"Is attending a celebration today in the Place D'Armes. When I saw him," Lafitte added, "he asked about you. He said he would visit you soon. He said you have a horse somewhere—in Tennessee, perhaps? And your horse and his horse are going to race when you both are home again."

He extended his hand. "Good-by, Lee."

He swallowed hard. "Good-by, sir. And faith, good luck!"

Captain Dominique You also shook hands. "Once I theenk I walk you on the plank to drown," he said guiltily. Then he brightened. "But lucky I don't, eh? So in thees battle when the Redcoat would keel me, you are there. You save my life. Ees maybe not worth much, but ees useful to me—eh? And now, my frien', adieu!"

It was Tennessee and May. The sun poured down on the sleek horses stretching their necks forward while their hoofs clattered dully on the mud track in a field of General Jackson's farm, The Hermitage.

Lee, bent forward over the whipping mane of Venus, felt her straining to go faster, yet faster. But he held the reins taut, out of the corners of his eyes watching alertly that low, stretching horse alongside. Truxton, greatest racer of them all, was back in form despite his five years. But Venus, after a slow, steady training over three weeks, also was at her best. And this was a race!

The moist dirt of the track flowed underfoot. Over along the rail on the opposite side of the oval track stood a thin line of watchers. That tall, narrow figure was General Jackson, his piercing gray eyes pinning the two horses battling the long stretch chest-to-chest.

And they were on even terms thus far. Venus, in good trim when Lee returned, was speeding faster now than ever she had as a two-year-old filly. Jackson's stablemen had taken good care of her, kept her running and resting and running again. So that today's race, so long planned, was a real sporting event between an unknown three-year-old and a world-famous racer nearing the end of his career.

"Don't get excited! There's time!"

At Lee's words the alert ears cocked back. Venus ceased fighting her bit and only sped steadily, holding her place beside the great Truxton. And Lee, wondering if she had re-learned her signals sufficiently for the test on the home-stretch, rehearsed in his mind how he would suddenly slack the reins, kick her gently.

It was the curve. Truxton's rider, experienced in many a race, had adroitly stolen the inside. There was nothing to do but let Venus out so as to keep up. Lee slackened the reins and she responded eagerly. Around the curved end of the track they swept . . . and now it was the final straightaway.

"*Venus!*" Lee shouted abruptly. At the same instant he slacked his reins, leaned far forward, and gave her his heels.

She responded like a suddenly released spring. She seemed almost to leap ahead into a faster, mightier stride. With his face stinging at the whipping mane-ends, his weight carefully held over her neck so as to pitch her forward—but not too much—Lee, through blurred, slitted eyes saw the ground roll underfoot.

Only seventy yards . . . but Truxton was thundering abreast still. Fifty yards . . . and now Venus had forged front by a nose. Lee's heart bounded with hope. He heard sharp commands from the other jockey, heard the smack of a whip. Truxton, stung,

They Thundered Down the Track

bounded forward, inching up even, then slightly ahead.

Forty yards . . . thirty . . . in desperation Lee gouged his heels at Venus. "Run, Venus! *Run!*"

The finish line swam at them. Abruptly it was gone, and the race was over. He did not know which horse had won, for the hard breathing Truxton had seemed exactly abreast. Or had there been a few inches advantage for one or the other?

When he had brought Venus to a halt and turned her, he saw Andrew Jackson on the track. Jackson ran to Truxton and held his nose a moment in affection and pride. As Lee came abreast he turned and caught Venus's rein. He stood stroking her muzzle and talking to her while Lee, mud-spattered and burning inside with anxiety, slipped to the ground.

"How was it, General?"

Jackson stared at him. "You don't know? Lee, my horse has been a great horse—one of the greatest racers of all time. But his day is gone, and this was his last race. And he didn't lose it, I'm proud to say! Though he didn't win, either."

"You mean—?"

Andrew Jackson laughed and clapped him on the shoulder. "I've never been tied before with Truxton —never. But those of us at the finish couldn't tell which was ahead. Their noses were in a line. Their chests were in a line. They are two great horses, lad. But mine is finished and ready for pasture the rest of his life. And yours—" Andrew Jackson's gray eyes twinkled. "Will you sell her?"

Lee swallowed. "No-o. I couldn't, sir. I just couldn't!"

"As I thought. But Lee, you're going to read law now, so you can be admitted to the bar and earn your living trying cases. When," he demanded, chuckling, "will you have time to race your Venus?"

Lee went to hold her head and stroke the velvety muzzle. Venus's ears cocked forward, and she nudged him with her nose the playful way she'd had long ago, before he went keelboating to adventure.

"Well, sir," Lee Baird admitted, "I mayn't have much freedom for racing Venus. But then, General Jackson, there'll be precious few horses fit to run with her. So 'twon't require much of my time!"